WAITING FOR DANG

"You'll catch it certain sure," he said when she joined him behind the rock. "I told you to bide at home like a..."

"Like a woman should," said Liza and made a face at him. "Please, Adam, don't tell Pa...."

"He'll likely find out for himself," said Adam. "Nothing much misses him. Settle here now and stay quiet." He pulled her down beside him, then sat back with his rifle across his knees.

Liza stole a sideways look at him, hoping to find that he really wasn't cross with her.

"Seen any rabbits yet?" she asked.

"Hush!" Adam put out a warning hand. "'Tisn't rabbits I'm after. I'm keeping my eye on the land." He was whispering but so softly that his words reached Liza like a fading echo.

Liza stared at him. He looked as though he were expecting something to happen, something bad. Her heart began to beat fast and her hands clenched.

"There!" Adam nodded toward the far edge of the clearing. "I was waiting for them. They're coming now."

LIZA
was originally published by Thomas Y. Crowell Company.

Critics' Corner:

"In the two years since her mother's death 12-year-old Liza had been torn two ways. Her own desire to live like a boy wearing blue jeans, hunting with her older brother, and roaming the hills was in direct conflict with her father's hope that she grow into a lady, taking full responsibility for the housekeeping and looking after the baby. A feud with the neighbors over selling off the timber and a flood bring matters to a climax in this three-dimensional story of Kentucky mountain people. Strong characterization and a warm family feeling make this better than the average story of a girl's growing toward maturity." —*Library Journal
(especially recommended)

"The relationships between Liza and her older brother, and between the girl and her father, are described with insight and clarity." —University of Chicago Bulletin of
the Center for Children's Books

"...extraordinarily clear perceptions of human nature, and with an outstanding ability to couch her story in convincing terms of its locale...." —Christian Science Monitor

"A warm story which gives the reader insight into an obscure but rich area of this country, this story by a veteran writer of juvenile fiction for all ages boasts an appealing heroine, a vivid background, and considerable action."

—Virginia Kirkus Service
(starred review)

Other Recommendations: Child Study Association of America.

About the Author:

ELISABETH HUBBARD LANSING lives in Southport, Connecticut, and is a busy woman indeed. She takes care of her four children, is active in community affairs, runs a large house, and still finds time to write. She also teaches at a writing school. Her many books are popular with young people for, to quote *The New York Times,* "Mrs. Lansing maintains throughout a respect for the intelligence of her readers."

LIZA

LIZA

(Original title:
Liza of the Hundredfold)

by
Elisabeth Hubbard Lansing

Illustrated by
Dorothy Bayley Morse

AN ARCHWAY PAPERBACK
POCKET BOOKS • NEW YORK

LIZA

Crowell edition published 1960

Archway Paperback edition published October, 1968
2nd printing....................November, 1973

L

Published by
POCKET BOOKS, a division of Simon & Schuster, Inc.,
630 Fifth Avenue, New York, N.Y.

Archway Paperback editions are distributed in the U.S.
by Simon & Schuster, Inc., 630 Fifth Avenue, New
York, N.Y. 10020, and in Canada by Simon & Schuster
of Canada, Ltd., Richmond Hill, Ontario, Canada.

Standard Book Number: 671-29338-9.
Library of Congress Catalog Card Number: 60-6239.
Printed in the U.S.A.

For Laura and Tommy Hill

LIZA

Chapter 1

THE latch on the back door clicked and Liza sat up in bed, wide-awake and listening. Her room was behind the cabin kitchen and she could hear everything that went on outside. If the click came again she would know that Adam was going off without her.

"He promised I'd go along next time he went hunting," she whispered. She leaned toward the window, her long braids falling forward on her shoulders.

The night was just beginning to lighten. Two pale stars showed in the square patch of sky beyond the window. They looked cold and far away. Liza shivered suddenly.

"Reckon I was hearing things," she told herself, pulling the patchwork quilt around her. The move-

1

ment made the corn husks in her mattress rustle, but the sound did not hide the rattle of the back door when it snapped shut.

Liza was out of bed and at the window in one bounding motion. The quilt still hung from her shoulders as she fumbled at the latch. It stuck and she jerked at it impatiently.

"Open up," she said in a fierce whisper. The latch gave and Liza thrust her head out the window. "Adam!"

Adam was there all right. She could see his tall shadow near the door and the rifle in his hand.

"You promised!" Her voice rose in a wail. "I'm coming. You said so."

"Hush now." Adam spoke gently. His voice was slow and careful. Adam was fifteen and already he talked like a man grown. He came toward the window, stepping quietly on the dry yard grass.

Liza could see his face now and she studied it intently to see if he remembered his promise. Every time Liza really looked at Adam she thought of their mother. She had been dead and gone for two years, but Liza remembered all the lines and curves of her face because Adam was so like her. He had the same narrow face and dark blue eyes. Even the way his black hair swept back from his forehead was the same.

Adam smiled and Liza's hopes rose. "I can ready myself right quick," she said. To show that she

2

meant what she said she caught up her braids and wound them around her head in a tangled bundle.

"Not this day," said Adam. "You know what Father said last night about your minding Seth like a woman should. You're not a woman growed but . . ."

"I'm twelve," said Liza. She straightened up to show how tall she was and bumped her head on the window frame. "Ouch!" Liza rubbed her head with both hands. "Seth's sleeping and nothing rouses him till it's time for breakfast."

Seth's small box bed was in the room behind her. He shared her sleeping space because he was only three years old and he was Liza's responsibility. But right now she didn't want to remember that she was supposed to watch out for Seth. She wanted to go hunting with Adam on the hills behind the cabin. It was early spring. The air smelt of damp earth and freshening green. Staying at home was no fun when she might be walking the hills in the rising morning light.

"Annie Lou can watch over him," she said urgently. "Adam, please!"

Adam shook his head. "Annie Lou's no use with the Least 'Un," he said firmly. "Leastways not to fix him for the day."

Liza knew that Adam was right. Annie Lou was their father's kin. She had lived with the family ever since Liza could remember. She could cook and sew patches, but she was too old to mind Seth.

"You promised certain sure," said Liza in a last desperate hope that Adam might change his mind.

He shook his head once more. "Hunting's not for girls," he said. "You know Father says that." Adam turned away and walked up the sloping yard toward the dark line of trees at the top of the garden patch.

"Not for girls!" Liza glared after Adam until he disappeared in the shadow of the trees. Then she set her mouth in a thin line. "I'm coming," she said aloud, "and you can't stop me, not you nor Father nor . . . nor anybody!"

Two minutes later Liza had pulled on an old pair of Adam's jeans and tucked her tangled braids into a cap that had once belonged to him. The

4

jeans were too long, but Liza rolled them hurriedly above her knees. She didn't bother with shoes. Unless it was really cold Liza never wore them. The soles of her feet were nearly as hard as leather and it was easier to run without shoes.

As she dressed, Liza thought about a brother who made a promise and then broke it. She remembered everything her father had said about her duties as a housekeeper and taking care of Seth. But she pushed his words to the back of her mind. It was better to think of Adam and the fun of going hunting.

"I'll be back in time to fix Seth for his breakfast," she said, glancing toward his bed. All she could see of him was a small mound of quilt and a handful of bright curls on the pillow.

Liza tiptoed toward the bed and bent over him. Now she could see one flushed cheek and the outline of his stubby nose. Sleeping or waking, Seth looked like a Christmas angel.

"Stay sleeping," she whispered and smoothed the quilt over his shoulders.

She went to the door leading into the kitchen and lifted the latch carefully. Beside the door was a chair and on the chair was the plaid cotton skirt she had taken off the night before. Liza looked down at the faded jeans. Then she looked at the skirt and sighed.

"I better wear it," she thought. "Father doesn't hold with pants for girls."

She yanked on the skirt, struggling to button it over the bulky jeans. If she didn't hurry, Adam would be too far up the mountain for her to catch up. But the button refused to go into the buttonhole. She searched frantically among the confusion of things on top of her chest of drawers. There were six colored stones, a robin's nest, a box of nails, and the skeleton of a squirrel on the chest, but no pins in sight. She found a safety pin at last under the box of nails and jabbed it into the skirt. As she worked the pin into the skirt folds she watched her reflection in the mirror over the chest. The big cap, bulging with her braids, nearly hid the blue of her eyes. But beneath its shadow she saw her sharp, upturned nose and the freckles scattered over it.

"You look like a boy anyway," she told herself and gave a satisfied nod.

Once again she lifted the latch of the kitchen door and went softly into the big room. It was dim and still in the early light. Liza could see the outline of the center table, the looming bulk of the great stone fireplace, and the glow of the rag carpet before the hearth. Beyond the fireplace was the door leading to her father's room.

She kept her eyes glued to that door as she crept toward the back. Her father was a heavy sleeper, but if he chanced to waken, all hope of going hunting was gone. She stepped on a loose floor board and stopped, her heart pounding. Then she risked a look at a door on the opposite wall. Annie Lou was sleeping behind that door. At least Liza hoped she was sleeping. But you never could tell about Annie Lou. She was old and surprising.

Liza took three long steps toward the back door and opened it with a hasty push. The hinge gave a hideous squeak and once again her heart jumped. But she didn't wait to see if the sound had wakened the sleepers. She snatched an old padded jacket from a peg beside the door and raced up the garden slope without looking back.

Once she stumbled on a dried turnip stump and saved herself from falling only by catching at the corner post of the pigsty.

"Whew!" Liza slipped out of sight behind the shed and stopped for breath. Inside the shed she could hear Old Ben, the mule, moving on his straw bed, the restless cluck of the hens, and a grunt from Tilda, the sow.

"Hush now," whispered Liza. "Too early for eating, you old pig, you."

Tilda was Liza's special pet, but her breakfast could wait. She pulled on the jacket, shivering in the sharp air. "Tisn't spring yet," she told Tilda, "no matter if it is April. Go back to sleep." She pat-

7

ted the side of the shed and turned toward the trees above the garden.

"Which way might he go?" she asked herself, remembering the many twisting paths that led along the mountain. She knew that Adam meant to get a rabbit this morning. He had told his father so the night before.

Liza started up the slope, half-running on the rough ground.

"There's rabbits in the cleared place and down in the hollow," she said aloud. "If he . . ." Liza stopped because she had to. Her skirt was caught on a briar.

Liza didn't waste words as she tore at the offending skirt. It came away from the briar with a long protesting rip, but she didn't look at the damage. She gathered the skirt folds in a bundle and stuffed them under the belt of her jeans. It made an uncomfortable bulge around her middle, but Liza didn't care. Now she could run without the bother of a skirt around her knees.

"He's gone to the clearing," she thought as she came within the shadow of the trees. "He's sure to rouse a rabbit there." She turned into a dark alley beneath the pines and climbed steadily toward the top of the mountain.

All this section of the hillside belonged to her father. It lay among the Middle Folds of the Hundredfold Hills, far in the back lands of the Kentucky mountains. Not more than a handful of people lived alongside the creek beds of the Middle Folds and the nearest neighbor was more than a mile away. But Liza had been in the hills all her life and had never known loneliness.

Now as she hurried along the path Liza took time to look about her at the dark pines and the slanting light on the needle-covered ground beneath them. Her father took pride in keeping his land cleared, even the wooded parts. During the winter months he and Adam chopped away the dead wood and underbrush, so that the trees stood tall and straight on the Mather property. The paths and trails were kept free too. Liza knew them all so well that she never once hesitated at a fork or turn as she followed after Adam.

Near the crest of the mountain Liza stopped and listened. Overhead was the soft whisper and rustle of the pines and far below in the hollow was the faint chuckling of Mather Creek as it wound and twisted over its stony bed. But these were old and expected sounds. Liza wanted to hear Adam's footsteps or the crack of his rifle.

"Adam!" Liza called his name just to hear a voice on the wide mountainside.

A gray squirrel on a branch over her head began to chatter, a shrill, loud sound in the morning air.

"You keep shut!" Liza threw a stick at him, but

he only whisked to another branch and scolded harder than ever.

"If I had a rifle like Adam I'd shoot you cold dead," said Liza. "You're good for nothing but stew."

Instantly Liza was hungry. She thought of the squirrel stews her mother used to make and the thin pale stuff that Annie Lou called a stew. Liza sighed. Annie Lou was too old to take trouble with the cooking and it was no use to think of her mother. The wasting sickness had taken her away and Liza had learned to push the sadness of thinking about her to the back of her mind. She made herself remember that she was looking for Adam.

"Adam!" This time she shouted his name, forgetting everything but the need of having him near. She began to run, calling his name with every breath.

At the edge of a clearing near the ridge she stopped. The sky was lighter now, and above the fringe of trees at the crest of the mountain was the reddening glow of the rising sun. It cast a pinkish light on the rocks and bushes in the clearing and Liza's spirits lifted. In the open space she felt safer and more sure of herself.

"I wasn't scared on the path," she said aloud. "Not one bit scared," she repeated to make it sound true.

"Boo!"

10

The sound came from behind a rock at the clearing's edge and Liza gave a startled shriek. The next moment she saw the top of Adam's cap above the rock and the muzzle of his rifle.

"Pooh," said Liza. She coughed to make her voice stop shaking.

Adam's long arm reached out and beckoned her to him. "You'll catch it certain sure," he said when she joined him behind the rock. "I told you to bide at home like a . . ."

"Like a woman should," said Liza and made a face at him. "Please, Adam, don't tell Pa . . . I mean Father." She remembered that her mother had taught her to say Father because it showed respect.

"He'll likely find out for himself," said Adam. "Nothing much misses him. Settle here now and stay quiet." He pulled her down beside him, then sat back with his rifle across his knees.

Liza stole a sideways look at him, hoping to find that he really wasn't cross with her. Adam had always been her friend, even if he was a boy and older than she. Now as she sat straight against the rock Liza saw that he was frowning and that his eyes had a queer look of waiting.

"Seen any rabbits yet?" she asked.

Adam didn't seem to hear. He bent forward, his hands gripping the rifle butt.

11

"Where's the rabbit?" Liza's voice rose in quick excitement.

"Hush!" Adam put out a warning hand. "Tisn't rabbits I'm after. I'm keeping my eye on the land." He was whispering but so softly that his words reached Liza like a fading echo.

Liza stared at him. Adam had strange ways sometimes, but she had never seen him act like this. He looked as though he were expecting something to happen, something bad. Her heart began to beat fast and her hands clenched.

"There!" Adam nodded toward the far edge of the clearing. "I was waiting for them. They're coming now."

"Them? Who's them?"

But Adam's hand closed over her mouth and Liza was quiet, waiting with him.

Chapter 2

THE four men who came into the clearing stopped near its center and stood in a group. They did not speak, but looked about them at the high surrounding trees.

Liza, her eyes bulging with interest, watched from the shelter of the rock. Adam's hand was still over her mouth. If it hadn't been, she knew she would have cried out with surprise. Three of the men were neighbors, men who lived in the same hollow. Liza had known them all her life and their families too.

There were only four families in Mather Hollow. The Lashers, the Bedfords, the Tillotsons, and the Mathers were friends as well as neighbors. They had to be because they depended on one another for help in time of trouble and for company in the loneliness of the hill country.

13

"Wh—— wh——?" Liza couldn't get her question through Adam's hand, but her eyes asked it for her as she nodded at the fourth man.

"Lumber Company," said Adam softly. He leaned forward, straining to hear what the men might say.

Liza remembered now that she had seen the stranger once before. He was the boss man of the Lumber Company that had brought its great saws and crew of men to the next hollow, where they were cutting the trees, ripping through the old pines and laying bare the land. Sometimes during the day when the wind was right she could hear the whine of the saws and the aching cry of the trees as they fell.

Liza jerked her head to one side to free herself from Adam's hand. Instantly she put her own hand over her mouth to show that she meant to be quiet. Adam gave her one warning look, then turned to watch the men once more. Liza did the same.

The Lumber Company man wore a plaid shirt and high leather boots. He was square and wide in the shoulders, very different from the neighboring men. They were tall and narrow like Liza's father and most of the men of the hills. Only Mr. Tillotson showed the effect of his wife's good cooking. His waistline was comfortably round.

"What are they doing?" asked Liza in a breath.

Adam didn't answer. He didn't even seem to

hear, for he was still watching and waiting. None of the men had spoken yet. They looked at each other and seemed to hope that someone else would do the talking. Liza saw Mr. Tillotson hunch his shoulders and look nervously over his shoulder at the path that led down to the Mather cabin. Mr. Lasher and Mr. Bedford watched the Lumber Company man, who stood with his hands on his hips, studying the trees at the edge of the clearing.

"Nice trees." The Lumber man had a hard, big voice that sounded like the pounding of rocks in the creek.

Liza jumped when he spoke and would have cried out if Adam had not nudged her into silence.

"Dan Mather's always been one to mind his trees," said Mr. Tillotson. He sighed as he spoke and Liza guessed he was thinking of his own wild, untended woodland.

"Pays off," said the Lumber man. "Easier to cut, better price." He gave the three men a sharp look. "Well?"

The question was like a bullet and it made his companions jump. Mr. Lasher shrugged but said nothing. He looked at Mr. Bedford and gestured for him to speak. Mr. Bedford scratched his head, coughed, and nodded at Mr. Tillotson. But Mr. Tillotson was scraping one foot against a stone. He didn't seem to notice that the others were all looking at him.

"The offer still holds," said the Lumber man. "I'll pay cash money for the trees. But not a cent to anyone, if I don't get a clean sweep of all the trees in the hollow. These Mather trees are the best of them and, if I can't get them, I ain't bothering to cut the others."

Mr. Tillotson groaned aloud. "Dan Mather ain't selling," he said mournfully. "He ain't selling for good cash money nor for gold."

Liza blinked. She remembered that Mr. Tillotson had come to the cabin two days ago just at the edge of dark. Her father had sent her out into the yard with Seth and she had not heard the two men talk. But Mr. Tillotson had gone off after a short time looking angry and uncomfortable. Her father had sat the whole evening, his face dark and troubled. But he hadn't spoken once about what Mr. Tillotson had said. Adam knew, for he had been allowed to stay and hear the talk. That was because he was a boy and not a girl who had to be sent out of the way when anything important or interesting happened.

Now she leaned toward Adam and whispered in his ear. "Was that why Father was so black mad after Mr. Tillotson came? Was it about selling the trees he came?"

Adam nodded but at the same time motioned her to be still.

Mr. Lasher and Mr. Bedford frowned when Mr.

Tillotson finished speaking. They looked uneasily at the Lumber man, but they found no words to say what they felt.

"Tain't natural," said Mr. Tillotson at last. "I put it up to Dan Mather just like you said. Two hundred dollars cash money for his trees, more'n you'd give any of the rest of us. He just sat there, dark as thunder, saying nothing. Just one word when I'd said all I could. He said no."

The Lumber man laughed but he didn't sound amused. "It's up to you. You got just ten days to get him to change his mind. We'll be finished cutting the next hollow then and I can't keep my gear and crew waiting on nobody. Once we leave we ain't coming back. It costs too much to move the outfit in. So it's now or never."

The three neighbors looked at each other, their faces anxious and grim.

"Ask Dan again," said Mr. Bedford, nodding at Mr. Tillotson. "I'd do it myself only you're a nearer neighbor to him than me." He hitched his belt higher, then jabbed at Mr. Tillotson's well-covered ribs to make himself clearer. "You tell him it's good cash money. Tell him that real plain, Sam Tillotson, and tell him the Lumber Company ain't buying any trees in the hollow if his trees can't be bought too."

"That's right," said Mr. Lasher. "Tell him plain."

Mr. Tillotson moved back to escape his neighbor's stabbing finger and heaved his shoulders in a helpless gesture. "Can try," he said uneasily, "but you know what Dan Mather's like. He ain't one to move with talk, not when he once says no."

"Well, it's up to you," said the Lumber man briskly. "You see to it and let me know. Ten days, mind. That's all the time you got." He turned his back on the three men and strode off toward the ridge. A minute later he had disappeared among the trees in the direction of the next hollow where his crew was working.

Liza watched him go, then looked back at the three neighbor men. Mr. Tillotson seemed more uncomfortable than before.

"Seems like I always got to be the one to face Dan Mather," he said finally. "You know he ain't a man you can be easy with."

"You get up your spirit and don't let Dan rile you," said Mr. Bedford. He slapped Mr. Tillotson encouragingly on the back. "Dan don't scare me none. It's kind of too bad I ain't got the spare time to talk to him myself. But you can talk him round, Sam, and as for letting Dan Mather overset you, just remember it's good cash money you're talking. For cash money there ain't a man in the hills wouldn't face the black one hisself." He clapped Mr. Tillotson once again on the shoulder.

"That's right," said Mr. Lasher.

The three men walked away together, their voices fading among the trees. Mr. Bedford did the talking. Mr. Lasher agreed with everything he said, and Mr. Tillotson, walking between them, only mumbled his replies.

Liza waited until the last echo of Mr. Bedford's voice floated up the mountainside. Then she turned accusingly to Adam. "You knew about the offer! Why didn't you tell me?"

Adam got slowly to his feet, his rifle in his hands. For a moment he looked at the place where the three neighbor men had been standing, his face set and pale.

"Tisn't right," he muttered.

"What isn't?" demanded Liza. She scrambled to her feet and planted herself squarely in front of Adam. "Why isn't it right? Why won't Father sell the trees? Two hundred dollars! Whew!" She whistled. "There's not that much cash money in the world."

Adam looked at her as though suddenly remembering that she was with him and had heard everything. "It's a power of money," he said slowly. "But Father's set his mind against it and there's no use to try and change it. He says it's against Nature to cut trees like the Lumber Company does, cleaning out a whole hollow like they do. Besides . . ." He stopped and sighed.

"Besides what?" said Liza. She was puzzled by

Adam's way of speaking. He sounded uneasy, almost as though he wasn't sure of his own thoughts.

"Mother liked these woods," said Adam. He smiled and instantly Liza knew that he was remembering their mother and how she had loved to walk the woods. She had known every tree on the mountainside; which ones had nests of birds and where the bloodroot grew beneath their branches. The dogwood she had loved especially and the hills were white with its flowers when it blossomed in the spring.

"I know," said Liza. "Is that why Father won't sell? Because Mother wouldn't want it so?"

"I reckon so in part," said Adam. "I can't tell what Father thinks. He doesn't say. It's like Mr. Tillotson said. He just said no with his face hard and angry-like. I wish . . . never mind." Adam hoisted his rifle to his shoulders and turned toward the ridge. "Come along now. We're hunting rabbit, don't forget."

Liza skipped along after him as he crossed the clearing toward the thin line of trees along the ridge. She didn't speak for several minutes, but her mind worked busily. Two hundred dollars! Liza thought of the things she could order from the Wish Book if the family had two hundred dollars in cash money. She looked at Adam's straight back, wondering if he felt as their father did or whether he would like the cash money too.

"What would you do?" she asked, taking two running steps to catch up with him.

Adam glanced down at her, his eyes filled with thought. "It's not my place to say," he said at last. "Watch that root! You'll fall and . . ."

But his warning came too late. Liza tripped over the root and fell flat among the pine needles. For a second she wanted to cry, for she had scratched one hand and all her breath seemed knocked out of her. Then in the next second she remembered that boys didn't cry. She clenched her teeth and let Adam pull her to her feet without making a sound.

"Hurt bad?" Adam leaned down to look into her face.

Liza sniffed. "No," she said loudly.

"Wouldn't say so anyhow," he said and smiled. "You should of been a boy, Liza. You're tough as oak timber."

Liza flushed with pleasure and her spirits leaped upward. "I'm as good as a boy any day," she said boastfully. "Bet I can beat you running to the top of the ridge."

Without waiting for Adam to accept her challenge, she set off up the slope at full speed, dodging among the trees and rocks like a running deer. She heard Adam pounding along behind her and knew he was getting nearer with every step. But the high rock that marked the top of the ridge was just ahead and Liza reached it with a mighty burst of speed a good three steps ahead of Adam.

"I done it! I done it!" she cried, her heart choking her with its rapid beating.

"Did it," said Adam. "Remember what Mother said."

Liza managed to nod as she fought to catch her breath. Her mother had been raised in the settlement at Hanford, twenty miles away on the outside. She had been to school and knew the ways of speaking among people who had book learning. She had brought her books with her when she married and came to live in the Hundredfold, so far away in the back hills. She had brought her gentle ways too and the housekeeping arts that had made the Mather cabin different from those of their neighbors. She had taught Adam and Liza to read because there was no school in the Middle Folds and she wanted her children to have learning.

"I forget right talking when I say things fast," said Liza when she could speak without panting.

"Don't," said Adam harshly. "We have to remember. There's no other way." He frowned and turned away.

Liza knew what he was thinking. Many times when they had talked together in the long months since their mother's death Adam had told her how he longed to keep on with his learning. There were only a handful of books in the cabin and Adam had read them all a dozen times. He read at night by the oil lamp and the books were old and ragged with reading. Liza knew that above all things in the world Adam wanted to go to school where there would be more books.

"If we had the cash money for the trees maybe you could go to school over Hanford way," she said softly, watching Adam's back.

"That's what I'm thinking," said Adam. "I can't stop thinking it, but it's no use."

"Why don't you talk to Father?" cried Liza, catching eagerly at his arm. "He'd listen to you because you're a boy. Talk to him real plain."

Adam had turned to Liza as she talked and for a moment his eyes lighted with hope. Then the hope faded and he shook his head. "Father's right about not cutting trees in a clean sweep," he said. "Look!"

He ran forward a few steps, pulling Liza after him. There on the high crest of the mountain they could look down into the next hollow. The Lumber Company had been at work here for more than a month and now they had nearly finished the cutting. Only a few misshapen trees, patches of underbrush, and the stark stumps of the cut trees were left on the bare, brown hillside. The creek wound its way along the floor of the valley, past the two cabins that were visible from the ridge.

"Seems kind of . . ." Liza stopped. She couldn't

find words for this wasted land. She shivered. "I wouldn't like our hollow to look this way," she said.

"Nor I," said Adam. "Father is right and I think his way. But I wish . . ." He looked down at Liza's solemn face and reached out to tweak up her cap brim. "Don't take on," he said. "We don't have need of cash money, not really. I just wish Mr. Tillotson and the others would see it Father's way too. They're fighting mad at him and it's not right for neighbors to act so."

Liza didn't answer. She followed Adam back toward the clearing and once again her thoughts crowded her head. She remembered the angry looks of the neighbor men when they spoke of her father. There was bound to be trouble among them if they held it against her father for not selling. She remembered something else too. The day before she had expected Emmy Tillotson to come and play with her and she had not come. Emmy was Liza's best friend. She was the only girl her age in the hollow and they had always been friends.

"I bet Emmy's pa wouldn't let her come," she said. "I bet Mr. Tillotson's so mad at Father he won't let Emmy play with me ever again." She looked anxiously at Adam.

Adam only shrugged. He wasn't really listening to Liza.

Liza sighed. It was bad enough to think that Emmy had deserted her. It was even worse to have Adam so far away in his thoughts that he wouldn't listen to her troubles. She kicked at a tussock of dried grass and felt sorry for herself. Maybe if she wasn't a girl things would be different. Then she could do things that boys did and be important.

Adam was several feet ahead of her now. He had forgotten all about her. He had even forgotten that he was supposed to be hunting, for his rifle was held carelessly in one hand and his eyes were watching the ground at his feet.

A leaping shadow crossed the path in front of them and Liza's quick eyes followed it. It was a rabbit, a big one, just right for a stew.

"Adam! Look, there's one! Get him! Get him!"

Liza forgot that hunters were supposed to be quiet. She ran toward Adam, shrieking at him to notice the rabbit. Before he could follow the direction of her pointing finger, she snatched the rifle and aimed it at the leaping rabbit. The rifle was big and Liza had fired it only a few times in her life. She tried to aim the wavering muzzle at the fast-moving target, but it was too heavy for her. Long before she had fixed the sights the rabbit had disappeared in the underbrush with a flaunting whisk of his stumpy tail.

"Drat!" Liza threw the rifle on the ground in a fury of disappointment. It hit a rock on the path and Liza stared at it in horror. The blow had broken the butt from the muzzle and the rifle lay in two pieces at her feet. It was Adam's dearest possession, the very pride of his life.

Chapter 3

LIZA trailed slowly after Adam down the slope of the yard. It was full daylight now. The sun was well up over the hills, warming away the chill of the early morning. She kicked through the dry clods of the garden plot, sending up a small sun-specked cloud before her.

Adam's back was toward her and she saw the two pieces of his rifle, one held in either hand. Liza shut her eyes and groaned.

"He won't listen. He won't say one breathing word," she whispered. She thought of the horrible moment when she saw the rifle lying on the ground. For a full minute she was so stricken at what she had done that she could only stare at the broken rifle, not daring to look at Adam.

When she had at last found her voice she had tried to tell him how she felt. She wanted to make him understand that she was sorry and that she knew what her angry gesture meant to him.

But Adam hadn't said a word. He hadn't even looked at her as he bent down to pick up the two pieces of his rifle. He had only taken them in his hands and walked away down the mountain toward home.

Liza had been left to follow after him, still apologizing, still saying over and over how sorry she was. Adam had not answered her. He didn't seem to hear her or even to know that she was near. But Liza had seen his face when he took the rifle in his hands and she knew exactly what he felt.

"I wisht I was dead," she said out loud. "If I was dead the rifle wouldn't be broken and Adam wouldn't look that way, saying nothing." A hard little sob escaped her and she held her breath. "Adam!" His name burst from her in a choking cry.

Adam was by the back door now and he turned to look at her. Liza ran forward and caught his arm. "I didn't mean no harm . . . I mean any . . . honest I didn't. Adam, you got to believe me."

"I know," said Adam slowly. "I know you didn't, but . . . Hist!" He nodded toward the cabin.

Liza heard the sounds that came from inside too. In the room where she slept Seth was crying, a forlorn moaning that meant he wanted to be noticed. From the kitchen came a slow and mournful singing that proved Annie Lou was up and fixing breakfast. She always sang the old hill songs as she worked, even though she had forgotten half the words and most of the tunes. Worst of all, Liza heard her father's voice. It was calling her name and it wanted an answer.

Liza gave Adam a despairing look. What would her father say when he knew that she had been out on the hills instead of doing her duty at home as a right-thinking girl should? She ought to have Seth all dressed by now. She ought to be helping Annie Lou. Most important of all, she ought to be dressed in a skirt, with her hands and face washed for the day.

"I'm going to catch it," she whispered. "Father's going to be fighting mad with me." She yanked off the padded jacket and flung it over the peg. Then she pulled the rumpled skirt away from her waist and tried to smooth it over her knees to cover the blue jeans. She looked bulky and mussed, but at least the telltale pants didn't show.

"I reckon I better call out to him," she said shakily.

"Reckon so," said Adam.

Liza cleared her throat and answered her father in a very small voice. She pushed open the back door and stepped into the cabin kitchen. As she passed Adam he reached out and snatched off the cap that covered her braids. They fell down on her shoulders and Liza only had time to give him a grateful look before she faced her father.

Dan Mather was a frightening man when he had cause to be angry. He was tall, with high narrow shoulders and a way of holding himself that made him look as though his backbone would never bend. His face was narrow too and a dark beard covered his chin. Only his eyes, a deep and brilliant blue, ever showed that he was a man of feeling and tenderness. But when he was angry his eyes were cold as stones and there was no light of warmth in them.

He was angry now. He stood stiff and straight by the kitchen table and watched Liza as she came slowly toward him. No word was spoken. Words weren't needed to say that he knew where she had been and what he thought of her unwomanly doings.

Liza stood before him with her head down. She couldn't meet her father's eyes so she looked at her feet instead. They were clotted with dust from the garden and scratched by the briars on the mountain. Out of the corners of her eyes she saw Annie Lou bent over the fireplace, stirring corn mush in an iron pot that hung from a crane.

Annie Lou wore her usual black cotton dress and her head was tied up in a woolen shawl. A few wisps of gray hair showed beneath the folds of the shawl. They hung about her thin, wrinkled face like strands of cotton. Her beaked nose and deep-set eyes made her look like a witch in a fairy tale. But Annie Lou was not a witch; she was only old with a forgetting mind and queer ways.

Liza tried to think about Annie Lou as she watched her. But every moment she felt the nearness of her father and his anger. It was as though the whole kitchen were filled with his unspoken words. At last he moved slightly and placed one hand on the table. It was a long hand, rough with work but strong and hard. Liza watched him dust a few crumbs from the table top. They were crumbs that Liza should have swept away the night before when supper was done. Her face grew hot and she turned her head away.

But everywhere she looked were signs of things she had not done. The floor was dusty, for she had forgotten to sweep it. In a corner was a heap of Seth's clothing that she had not picked up. When her mother was alive the kitchen had shone with neatness and sparkled with the scrubbings she gave it. Now it was dreary with disorder and it was Liza's fault for letting it be so. She closed her eyes and sighed.

"Seth's crying," said Adam quietly. He had come into the kitchen with no one noticing him and stood just behind Liza. "I let her come hunting with me," he added, looking straight at his father.

Liza gasped, but before she could protest Dan

Mather began to speak. He said the things that Liza had known he would say. He spoke of her tangled hair and rumpled skirt. He pointed to her scratched and dirty feet and the stains on her hands and arms. All these things, he said, were not fitting for a girl.

"Hunting is boy's work," said Dan Mather. He had a slow way of talking that made all his words important.

A tiny spark of anger jumped into Liza's heart. Boys could do anything. They could go hunting and they could listen to the grown folk talk when there were interesting things to be said. Girls had to stay at home and cook and sew and scrub. They had to mind the Least 'Un and listen to old women and their wandering talk.

It was on the tip of her tongue to say what she thought of a girl's duties, but Adam reached out and touched her hand in a warning gesture. Liza shut her mouth tight to keep the words back.

"Ain't no way fer a girl to be. Ain't nothin' but trouble a-comin' from her wild ways." Annie Lou's voice was cracked and thin but it sounded loud in the room.

Liza frowned at Annie Lou, who was shaking her head as she stirred the mush.

"I'm not wild," said Liza resentfully.

"Hawks is wild," said Annie Lou. "Wild in the air and flyin' . . ." Her words trailed off in a mumble.

Liza shivered. Sometimes Annie Lou sounded almost crazy the way she talked.

"Liza." Dan Mather's voice was suddenly gentle. He reached out and lifted her chin so that she had to look at him. His eyes had lost their stony coldness. "Liza," he said again, "will you try to think on your mother's ways?"

"Father!"

Liza hurled herself at him and wrapped her arms tight about his waist. "I won't forget again," she cried. "I won't, I won't! I'll red up the cabin like she did and mind Seth . . . and . . ."

Her father patted her shoulder as she stumbled to a stop. "It's what's needed," he said. "It's not what it was, with no woman's touch."

"I'll make it so," said Liza eagerly. Now that her father was gentle with her she was ready to promise anything. She couldn't bear to have him stern and looking at her with hard eyes. She even forgot to remember that boys had all the fun as she hugged him again.

"Save me breath," he said and took her hands in his, looking at them for a moment. "A woman's touch has clean hands," he said.

Liza snatched her hands away and wrapped them in the folds of her skirt. "They've not been washed yet," she muttered. She backed away toward her room, still hiding her hands in her skirt. "I'll be getting Seth up and . . ."

"Fetch her in!" cried Annie Lou suddenly. She turned from the hearth and shuffled toward the table with a bowl of mush in her hands. "Fetch her in off the hills fer to come to the table."

Liza looked quickly at her father. She knew that it saddened him when Annie Lou talked this way. When she was upset she wandered in her mind more than usual. Then she believed that Liza's mother was out walking on the mountainside and would come back if she were called.

Now Liza saw the look she dreaded most come

into her father's face. It was a look so sorrowful that she could not bear to see it. She saw Adam reach toward his father as though to comfort him. But Dan Mather turned abruptly away and sat down at the table.

"Fetch up Seth," he told Liza in a hard voice. "Wash yourself like a woman should before she eats."

Liza didn't answer. The friendly warmth was gone out of the room and it was all Annie Lou's fault. Liza glared at her, wishing she dared tell her to be quiet and mind her own business.

"Go now, Liza."

Adam's quiet words made Liza remember that Seth was still crying in his bed and that her hands were still dirty. She went into her room, closing the door behind her to shut out the gloom and disorder of the kitchen. Seth's bed was near the door and Liza snatched him up, hugging him with all her strength.

"Hush now, hush," she murmured. "Liza's here."

Seth's round face was streaked with tears and his mouth was open for another wail. Liza put her hand over his mouth just in time. "Be still," she said.

Seth's blue eyes watched her solemnly. They were like drowned gentians behind his tears.

"Going to be quiet?" asked Liza, kissing him.

Seth nodded and Liza took ner hand away. "Teth cwy," he announced.

"Don't cry any more and I'll . . . I'll let you feed Tilda." Liza set Seth down on the rag carpet and began pulling off his night clothes. "All right?"

"Feeda Tilda!" he shouted and began to jump to show what he felt about the joyful prospect of feeding the pig. His bright curls bounced and his face grew scarlet.

"Stay still, you monkey!" Liza grabbed at him and shoved his fat legs into his overalls. It was like dressing a scared rabbit to get Seth into his clothes. She had to hold him tight between her knees to get his shirt over his head and wash his hands and face.

"Wiza dirty," said Seth when the struggle was over and he was fully clothed and ready for the day. He stood on the rug and looked at her critically with his head on one side. "Wiza face berry dirty."

"You don't have to tell me that," said Liza. "Everybody's been saying nothing else all morning. You be quiet!" She dumped more water from her night pitcher into the tin basin and began to scrub vigorously.

She hurried, for she knew her father was waiting at the table. He never wanted to eat a meal until the family was gathered. Then he said grace and they could eat.

When she finished her hasty wash she looked at

herself in the mirror. Her face was shining but her hair looked worse than ever. One braid had come loose and the other was frayed and matted. But there was nothing she could do about her hair until Annie Lou had time to braid it afresh. She tied a bandana over her head and tucked her braids under it.

"There!" she said and instantly forgot about her hair.

When she and Seth came into the kitchen her father and Adam were waiting. No one said anything as Liza lifted Seth into his chair and tied a napkin under his chin. But Liza could tell from the way they stared at their plates that her father and Adam had been talking. Adam had probably been telling about the neighbor men who had come to look at the Mather trees with the Lumber man. She glanced at him as she sat down by Seth and he shook his head at her.

"Annie Lou, are you setting with us this day?" asked Dan Mather.

Annie Lou didn't answer. She was rocking and singing softly to herself. Annie Lou seldom ate her meals with the family. She liked to keep her food in little plates and dishes near her chair. All day long she took bites and sups when she felt hungry. Some things she kept in a bag made of patchwork scraps, tied to the spindles of the chair. Annie Lou didn't take up much room in the big chair and there was plenty of space for the treasures she liked to have around her.

Even though no one expected Annie Lou to come to the table, Dan Mather never forgot to ask her.

"She's eating already," said Liza, who could see Annie Lou's jaws moving. She wanted her father to hurry with the grace, for she knew she couldn't keep Seth quiet much longer. He had already snatched up a spoon and was reaching for his bowl.

Liza caught Seth's hands in a tight grip as she bent her head. Seth opened his mouth to protest, but she poked a piece of biscuit into it before any sound came out.

Dan Mather began to pray. He mentioned all the family blessings and all the things for which he was grateful. "And may Eliza's soul rest in peace," he said at last.

He always ended his morning prayer by remembering his wife. Sometimes it gave Liza a start to hear her name mentioned in speaking to God. It reminded her that she ought to be more like her mother since she was named after her.

But this morning Liza had no time to think about her mother, for Seth pulled his hands away from hers and began drumming on the table with his spoon.

"Teth hungry," he shouted. "Teth eat now."

Liza pushed his bowl toward him and a moment

later the only sound in the room was the creak of Annie Lou's rocker and the splashing noises Seth made when he ate. Liza watched Adam and her father as she spooned up her mush. She hated mush and Annie Lou cooked it every morning. But now she was too busy hoping the men would say something interesting to care what she ate.

"Thought you went hunting for rabbit this morning," said Dan Mather, stirring his lumpy breakfast. He didn't care for mush either, not every day in the week. "Rabbit stew would taste mighty good."

"Rifle broke," said Adam. "Stock came clean away."

Dan frowned. He stopped eating and looked hard at Adam. A broken rifle would have to be mended at the blacksmith's. It would cost money and there was very little cash money to spare in the Mather household. Dan didn't have to say these things out loud. His eyes and his frown said them for him.

Liza made a sound in her throat. She didn't want Adam blamed for something that was her fault. But it was hard to get the words out and she cleared her throat again. "I . . . I didn't mean . . ."

"It hit against a rock," said Adam loudly. "It was pure accident."

Liza stared at him. A warm feeling of gratitude swelled inside her. She knew Adam didn't want her to get into any more trouble with her father. Suddenly her eyes were hot with tears. Luckily Seth dropped his spoon at that moment and Liza could wipe away her tears under the table where no one could see her.

Dan Mather said nothing more about the broken rifle until he had finished eating. Then he pushed back his chair. "Poor time for a broken rifle," he said. "With outsiders trespassing on the land we might have use for it. Get it fixed right quick."

Adam nodded. He knew what his father meant about needing the rifle. Liza did too, but she wanted to hear for herself what her father would do about the Lumber man.

"Would you shoot him?" she asked eagerly. "Shoot to kill?"

"Be quiet," said Adam. He nodded toward Annie Lou, who had stopped rocking and begun to moan softly at this threat of trouble.

"I'm not talking about shooting to kill," said Dan. "I'm talking of trespassing by outsiders, them that come on the land without so much as a by-your-leave." His face darkened. "Him and his cash money. Sam Tillotson should know better, and the others in the hollow too." Dan pounded the table with his hard fist. "Just let him come to me, that's all. You let me know right off if he comes. Hear?" He looked from Adam to Liza.

"Yessir," said Adam and Liza both at once.

They knew their father meant what he said. Even if he didn't shoot to kill, he wasn't going to have trespassers on his land.

Liza's heart skipped with excitement. She almost hoped the Lumber man would come. It would stir things up considerably if he did.

Later that morning when Adam and Dan had gone off about their men's business, Liza sat by the hearth while Annie Lou braided her hair. She hated to have her hair braided. Annie Lou was old, but her hands were strong and she pulled hard at every hair on Liza's head. It took a long time to make the braids smooth and by the time Annie Lou had finished, Liza's scalp was tingling.

"Ouch!" said Liza as Annie Lou raked the comb through the knots.

Seth laughed. He loved to watch Annie Lou comb Liza's long hair. Sometimes he helped by pulling at it or pretending it was a curtain to hide behind. But this morning Liza didn't want Seth bothering. She gave him his corncob baby to play with and sent him to his corner of the room.

Liza wanted to think about the Lumber man and the exciting possibility of his being shot at. She didn't dare talk about him to Annie Lou. It would upset her and make her wander in her mind again. Now that all was peaceful in the cabin, Annie Lou was sensible and could talk about everyday things.

"Adam's nice," said Liza, thinking of how he

had saved her from her father's anger. Then she sighed. "He's lucky being a boy."

"Boys is boys and girls is girls," said Annie Lou placidly.

"But boys have all the fun," said Liza.

Annie Lou sniffed. "Workin' all day and readin' all night like Adam is fun, you say!" She gave Liza's braid a sharp tweak. Annie Lou didn't hold with book learning. Sometimes when Adam was reading she would mutter to herself as though she thought he were doing the devil's work.

Liza knew enough not to talk about books to Annie Lou. She also knew that it was no use to say she hated housework. Annie Lou was of the old times. She thought girls should stay at home and be content.

She looked at the shelf where Adam kept his books. He had glued and mended them but still they were worn with reading. Sometimes Liza felt guilty when she looked at the books. She didn't read them the way Adam did. It was hard to sit still in a chair and do nothing but turn the pages of a book.

Liza stopped thinking about the books and watched Seth as he rolled on the floor. He was so round he was like a ball and could roll from end to end of the kitchen without stopping.

"Hit's plumb dirty, that floor," said Annie Lou

suddenly. "Iffen my bones was limber I'd wash it. Seems like young bones could . . "

"Seth!"

Liza was grateful to Seth. He bumped his head against the table leg and gave a convenient roar just in time to drown out the uncomfortable subject of the dirty floor. Liza ran to pick him up and by the time she had soothed his hurt, her hair was done and the floor forgotten.

"Reckon I'll run over and see why Emmy didn't come yesterday like she promised," said Liza. "I can take Seth."

Annie Lou was sleepy now. She was nodding in her chair and didn't seem to hear Liza. It took only a minute to bundle Seth into a jacket and escape out the door. Liza saw the heap of unwashed clothes in the corner and the breakfast dishes still on the table as she hurried out of the room.

"I can do the cleaning up later," she said as she ran across the yard to the gate. "Emmy might be sick. I ought to be neighborly and go see her."

Seth trotted after her, perfectly happy to be on the move. They scrambled down the steep path that led from the yard gate to the creek. Once on the winding path that followed the curves and twists of the stream bed they made quick time. Liza liked to run just as Seth did. It was a cool, bright day. The water raced and chuckled in the creek, a redbird flicked in a tree overhead.

Liza thought of the stuffy cabin, the heap of dirty clothes and the broom behind the door. It was no wonder she wanted to be here in the outside world instead of doing woman's work at home. She ran faster, her heart singing with the brook.

"Wait! Wait for Teth!" Seth's voice came in a wailing cry from behind.

Liza stopped. She was just beneath a high bluff at the edge of her father's land. A great wall of rock rose behind her and at its top was a flat table of ground, carpeted with moss and small growing things. The first bloodroot grew on the bluff and Liza remembered how her mother had taken her to hunt for the pale flowers in the spring before she died.

"They'll be blossoming now," said Liza. "We'll go find some tomorrow, Seth."

"Finda," said Seth who was prepared for anything now he had caught up with Liza. His face was red with running and his chest heaved.

"I'll carry you," said Liza, picking him up. "We've got to cross the log bridge and it's better so."

Seth had no objection to being carried and rested heavily on her shoulder as Liza walked toward the bridge. The overhanging bluff made it necessary to cross the creek at this spot and a few logs rested on the rocks to make a bridge. Liza stepped on the center log and started to cross. She had to be careful, for the logs were shaky and Seth was like a meal sack in her arms.

"Stay quiet," she told him.

"Quite," said Seth and jerked his legs to show that he meant to do as she told him.

Liza grabbed at him, the log rolled under her feet, and in the next moment she and Seth were in the water. It was deep and full by the bridge. As the water came over her head and shut out the light, Liza felt Seth slip away from her.

Chapter 4

LIZA's nose and throat and ears were choked with water. It blinded her eyes so that everything was black in the tumbling world of the creek. She had no time to be afraid. There was no time for anything but fighting the water. In her mind there was only one terrible thought. Where was Seth?

She reached and stretched her arms, feeling nothing but the yielding water or the jagged rocks of the creek bed. She came to the surface at last. Her lungs ached and her breath came in tearing gasps. It was hard to make things clear. There were dark shapes that must be rocks. But they moved past her, dipping and disappearing as the water carried her along.

Liza could not swim. She only knew that she must keep her arms moving. The motion kept her above water some of the time.

"Seth!" She meant to call out in a mighty shout. But all she heard was a croaking cry. "Seth, oh, Seth, where are you?" She spoke inside herself now. It was no use to shout. Her breath was gone and her throat was tight with fear.

Something bumped against her and Liza clutched at it. It was hard and knobby and Liza knew she was holding a log of wood. She clung to it desperately. The log floated and held her clear above the water.

Liza blinked, trying to see everywhere and everything at once. Seth must be near. He had to be. A moment later Liza and the log crashed against a rock. The blow shook the last bit of breath from her body and jerked the log from her hold. She clawed at the rock, her fingers scraping and grabbing for a grip on its rough surface. She felt a tiny ledge and hung on, half out of water and too tired to fight any longer.

For a time she was conscious of nothing but the rush of water about her legs and the blessed fact that she was holding onto something solid. When she could breathe without gasping, she began to shout.

"Seth!" It was a loud cry this time and it rang above the water sounds.

"I here. Teth all wet."

Liza's heart almost stopped. Seth's voice came from nearby. He sounded just as usual and a little cross. She turned her head to left and right. But there was nothing to see except the tumbling water on one side and the gray rock on the other.

The next instant she felt a hand on her shoulder. It held her strongly and pulled. She was on dry land, safe from the tug and terror of the water.

Seth was beside her. He was soaking wet, muddy, and red in the face. But he was alive, just as she was. He poked a finger at her.

"Wiza wet," he said.

"You're both wet."

The voice came from behind them. When she turned to look she saw a tall man standing there. Even in the first quick sight of him, Liza knew two things about him. He was kind and he was an outsider. She knew he was kind because his eyes and smile said so. He was an outsider because the men of the hills didn't wear store-bought clothes and this man did.

"Lucky I came by when I did," said the stranger. His voice was slow and easy. He talked the way Liza's mother had; like a person with book learning.

"Yes," said Liza shakily. Her breathing was still too uncertain for more words.

"I saw something red in the water and fished it out. I gather its name is Seth." The man leaned over Seth and began wringing water from his red jacket. "You all right now?" he asked Liza. "Sorry

I couldn't get to you sooner. You were under water most of the time." He smiled once more.

"I reckon so," said Liza and shuddered. Her chest didn't ache so much now and she was beginning to breathe more naturally. Then she remembered her manners. "Thank you," she said.

"Ank oo," said Seth, who liked to say the things Liza did. He smiled at the man. "Teth inna water."

"You weren't there long, old man," said the stranger cheerfully. "I got you out almost before you got your hair wet." He rubbed Seth's curls with a browned, long-fingered hand. "You better get him home," he said, nodding at Liza. "This is no weather for swimming."

Liza realized that she was shivering and that her clothes hung about her in a sodden, chilly mass. Long streams of water trickled off her braids. She jumped to her feet and reached out to lift Seth.

"I'll carry him," said the man and had Seth on his shoulder before Liza could protest. "Where do you live? Lead the way and I'll follow."

Liza started forward, then stopped. A fearful thought had come to her. Suppose her father had come home? What would he say to her for letting Seth fall in the creek?

"The Tillotsons!" she cried in a rush of relief. The Tillotson cabin was only a little farther away than her own house. Mrs. Tillotson was fat and cheerful. She wouldn't be angry if two wet and

soggy neighbors appeared at her door. There were six little Tillotsons and she was used to unexpected happenings.

"The Tillotsons are near," she said, talking fast so the stranger wouldn't ask where she lived.

"Run for it if you can," he said. "It'll warm you up."

So Liza ran for it. Her bare feet raced along the creek path. The stranger followed at a slower pace, for he did not know the stony path so well. Besides, Seth was drumming a tattoo on his chest with both feet, shouting approval of this delightful way of traveling.

Beyond the bluff was a great rock balanced at the edge of the water. It was a dark mass of stone, dividing Mather Creek from a smaller branch that led into a deep gulch between towering cliffs of black rock.

"Some rock!" shouted the man as Liza dodged beneath its shadow.

"The Devil's Seesaw," said Liza, who was glad to stop for rest and conversation. "Some say that once the Seesaw falls there's trouble coming."

"It won't fall easily," he said and shifted Seth to his other shoulder.

"That's T'Other Place down there," said Liza, pointing to the dark gulch. "It's real scary in there, all black and cold."

"You're shivering," said the stranger putting one

hand on Liza's shaking shoulder. "We better move along."

Nearly half a mile beyond the Devil's Seesaw was the Tillotson land. The Tillotsons lived in a sprawling cabin near the creek with a cluttered yard rising on the hillside behind it. Everything about the Tillotsons was sprawling and cluttered: the cabin, the yard, and even the family itself. As Liza picked her way through the litter in the front yard, she heard the cheerful shouts of the Tillotsons within the cabin.

"Sounds pretty lively," said the man. "I'll let you take Seth now. I don't want to disturb your neighbors." He put Seth into her arms, then nodded in farewell. "We may meet again. I'll be around here for a while."

Liza looked up at him. Suddenly she didn't know what to say to thank him for his help and kindness. But Seth needed no words. He lurched forward and threw his arms about the man's neck.

The stranger laughed and hugged Seth in return. "Thank you," he said and turned away.

"I . . . I . . ." Liza found her voice at last. "I'm real grateful to you," she shouted after him.

He waved from the yard gate. "By the way," he said as he closed the gate behind him, "do you know where Dan Mather lives? I want to see him."

A quick fear made Liza tighten her hold on Seth. The man must be from the Lumber Company. If he came near her father, there was no telling what might happen to him. She remembered what her father had said about trespassers and she thought of the rifle. This stranger with the kind ways had helped her. He mustn't know where Dan Mather lived.

These thoughts tumbled through her mind in a hurried blur as she stared toward the gate. Then on an impulse she turned and ran for the Tillotsons' cabin. She heard the stranger call out once, but when she reached the porch and looked back he was gone. Liza drew a long thankful breath as she opened the Tillotsons' door.

They were all there in the big untidy kitchen: all the Tillotsons, two dogs, and a family of cats. Mrs. Tillotson sat by the fireplace peeling potatoes from a huge bowl in her lap. She sang as she worked, a loud and lusty hill ballad that rose tunefully above the other noises in the room.

Two small Tillotsons rolled on the floor near her feet in a wrestling match that involved a wild flailing of arms and legs and a great deal of untuneful shouting. Two larger Tillotsons were washing one of the dogs in a tub of suds under the center table. The dog objected on a long note of complaint and his mate barked sympathetically from a corner.

The Least 'Un lay in a basket on top of the table, safe from the stirring activity around him. Emmy sat near to mind him. But the Wish Book was spread on the table before her and she was plainly more interested in its bright, promising pages than in the baby's cries.

For a moment no one noticed Liza standing in the doorway with Seth in her arms. Then as she stepped forward the sound and confusion was still. Seven pairs of eyes stared at her. Seven mouths fell open and stayed that way for two full seconds.

"Lawks a-mercy!"

Mrs. Tillotson was the first to recover from her surprise. Her voice broke the spell of silence and the noise began again on a louder and more active scale. Liza and Seth were surrounded by a swarm of Tillotsons, all shouting and pulling at Liza to make her explain herself. Only the Least 'Un stayed where he was. But his waving feet seemed to show that he would join the throng if he could.

"Stand back! Leave her be!"

Mrs. Tillotson heaved her bulk out of her chair and advanced on the group with firm authority. She pushed the children aside with a sweep of both arms and snatched Seth from Liza. She didn't have to be told what had happened and she knew just what to do.

"Git a quilt," she told Emmy. "Git dry things and warm 'em by the fire. Git now!"

As she gave her orders Mrs. Tillotson carried Seth to her chair by the hearth. She stripped his wet clothes away and began rubbing his round little body with both hands. The small Tillotsons crowded near to watch her. Even the two dogs pressed forward to look and the mother cat lifted her head from a basket.

Liza sat by the fire and shivered. She didn't try to talk. It was enough for her to sit still and let the fire's warmth get into her bones.

"Git dry things for Liza too," said Mrs. Tillotson when Emmy brought the quilt for Seth. "Take her off to the back room and git her dried out."

"Yes, Ma," said Emmy. She smiled at Liza. Emmy was fair and plump like her mother and all the other Tillotsons. Her face was round and her eyes were wide and blue. She wore her soft blond hair in two neat pigtails. Her dress was always clean and she liked to keep house and mind the Least 'Un. She was Liza's best friend in spite of all these things, for Emmy did everything that Liza told her to do and she never had ideas of her own.

"You fell in the creek," said Emmy when she and Liza were alone in the back room. She stared at Liza as though she couldn't imagine how anyone could be so venturesome as to fall in the creek and still be alive to tell about it.

Liza told what had happened as she hurried out of her wet things and into a dress of Emmy's. She didn't mention the outsider. It was more exciting to pretend that she had gotten Seth and herself out of the creek by her own efforts. Besides, she didn't want to talk about the man from the Lumber Company, now that her father and Mr. Tillotson were unfriendly about selling the trees. It was an uncomfortable subject.

"I'd of drowned dead," said Emmy admiringly when Liza had made the most of the dangers of the creek. "I'd of hated to get all wet and spoil my dress." She smoothed her starched skirt with her soft white hands.

"Pooh," said Liza, yanking at the skirt Emmy had given her to wear. It was much too big for her wiry figure, but Liza tucked it around her waist with a few hasty pokes. "I can swim, you know—almost, anyhow," she added in a burst of truth.

"Girls don't swim," said Emmy. "Hit's fer boys. Swimming gets your hair wet and mussy." She patted her tidy braids and looked hard at the bedraggled ropes of wet hair that hung on Liza's shoulders.

"It'll dry if I set by the fire a piece," said Liza carelessly. "Why didn't you come to play yesterday like you promised?"

Emmy's pink cheeks grew pinker. She looked pleadingly at Liza as though asking her not to make her speak.

"You promised certain sure," said Liza accusingly.

"Hit's Pa," said Emmy in a whisper. "He's real mad at your pa and taking on something awful." She shuddered. "Hit's not my fault," she said plaintively. "I asked him real nice if I could go to your house, but he says none of us Tillotsons can . . ."

"Emmy!"

Mrs. Tillotson's commanding voice cut Emmy off short. She finished her explanation with a helpless gesture of both hands.

"Don't take on," said Liza who could see that Emmy was ready to cry. "But I sure wish . . ."

"Emmy, you git Liza out here by the fire!"

Two seconds later Liza was sitting by the hearth. Seth, warm and dry in the quilt, lay sleepily quiet on Mrs. Tillotson's wide lap.

All the young Tillotsons crowded near, ready to hear Liza's story. She repeated it for her larger audience with several exciting additions that could easily happen to anyone who fell in Mather Creek. Emmy's eyes grew rounder with surprise and the little Tillotsons listened in wonderful silence.

"Hit's the Lord's mercy you wasn't drowned," said Mrs. Tillotson. "You acted right smart, Liza, saving Seth like you did. Your pa will be real proud."

"Don't tell him," said Liza quickly.

Mrs. Tillotson sighed. "Tain't likely I'll be talking with Dan Mather these days. My Sam's real angry with him and so's the other men in the hollow." She shook her head and heaved another sigh.

All the little Tillotsons looked at their mother and at Liza, their faces bright with excitement. Only Emmy, who was studying the Wish Book once more, sighed as her mother did. But it was hard to tell whether she was sighing for the treasures before her or for the trouble brewing in the hollow.

"He's made up his mind not to sell," said Liza. "There's no use to try to change him."

"Sam's got his mind set too," said Mrs. Tillotson. "I never seen him so set before. Selling them trees is meat and drink to him and to the others too. Hit's only your pa that keeps 'em from the cash money the Lumber Company is offering. I dunno. I just don't . . ."

She stopped as a small scuffling began among her brood, all of whom wanted to be nearest the center of talk and interest. Mrs. Tillotson quickly settled the argument by sending them all outside with one shouted "git."

With Emmy and the Least 'Un the only young Tillotsons left inside, and Seth sleeping in Mrs. Tillotson's lap, the kitchen became quiet. Liza stared into the fire, thinking of what Mrs. Tillotson had said.

"Are you set on selling?" she asked, for she had

caught the uncertainty in Mrs. Tillotson's last words.

"I can't put my mind on what to think," said Mrs. Tillotson. "Somehow it don't seem right to cut trees clean away. But Sam is thinking only about the cash money. I can't talk sense into him." Mrs. Tillotson shook her head disapprovingly. It was plain that she could generally "talk sense" into her husband.

"Think of the things we could order up from the Wish Book if we had cash money," said Emmy. "I hear tell the folks over in the next hollow are ordering up all they want with the money from the Lumber Company."

"Cash money's not everything," said Mrs. Tillotson sharply. "You mind your own affairs, Emmy."

"Yes'm," said Emmy. But she still looked longingly at the page of pretty dresses in the book open before her.

"I'd order up a pair of jeans, real ones," said Liza. "Then I wouldn't have to wear Adam's old pants."

"What would your ma say if she knew you was set on boy's pants?" demanded Mrs. Tillotson. "She was most like a lady of anyone I ever did know, real gentle and kind."

Liza didn't answer. It was never any use to talk about wishing she were a boy. Nobody understood or sympathized with her.

"I sure miss your ma," said Mrs. Tillotson. "She was always first here when my time came with the babies, helping in all ways. She was real neighborly. I've been thinking none of this un-neighborly way of acting would happen, if she was here. She wouldn't let the trees be cut. She loved 'em too well. That's why your pa won't sell now, I'm certain sure."

Liza nodded. "That's what Adam says."

"Hit nearly killed your pa when the wasting sickness took her off. He's not the same man since, uncertain in his temper like he is."

"I know," said Liza, remembering her father's deep silences and sudden angers.

"You should think on it," said Mrs. Tillotson. "Try to make it up to him by acting like a woman should, not wishing for boy's pants and all. You ought to . . ."

"My hair's dry," said Liza, who had heard this lecture before. "We had best get on home. I got things to do in the house."

Mrs. Tillotson smiled, but she helped dress Seth in his own clothes, which were now quite dry. She didn't mention Liza's womanly duties again and Liza was careful not to speak of the jeans she wanted.

Just as Liza finished getting into her own clothes a shout from the young Tillotsons announced that their father was coming in at the yard gate.

"He shouldn't find you here," said Mrs. Tillotson hurriedly. "Hit won't do to vex him more. You and Seth git along out through the back."

Liza was only too glad not to meet Sam Tillotson face to face. She bundled Seth into her arms and ran for the back door which Mrs. Tillotson held open for her.

"Thank you," she remembered to say as she pushed past Mrs. Tillotson. "I'm real grateful."

"Hit's just the neighborly way," said Mrs. Tillotson.

"Good-bye," said Emmy, who stood in her mother's shadow, looking after Liza with mournful eyes.

"I'll see you real soon," said Liza. Then she realized she wasn't likely to see Emmy soon or even ever again unless her father and Mr. Tillotson were friendly once more. Her arms tightened on Seth in a quick, hard hold.

"Hurting Teth," he protested.

"Everything's hurting," said Liza as she climbed the garden slope to the path that led along the mountainside toward home.

Chapter 5

"Lo . . o . . ok do . . wn, lo . . o . . ok do . . wn that lo . . o . . nesome road."

Liza sang the old song, dragging out the words in a doleful wail. She jabbed her needle into the patchwork square and looked at Annie Lou from under her eyebrows. Sometimes if she sang long enough she could make Annie Lou go to sleep. Once Annie Lou was asleep, Liza could put aside her sewing and escape into the wind and sunshine outside.

"Stitchin' too big."

Annie Lou was wide-awake. She sat across the hearth from Liza, bundled into her cluttered chair like a blackbird in its nest. Annie Lou was sewing too. Her patchwork quilts were famous for their stitching and their truth to the old patterns. Annie Lou kept dozens of the old designs in her head and she was teaching Liza to know them too. They were making the Sassafras Leaf quilt now. There were hundreds of tiny squares in the Sassafras Leaf and Liza was sure they would never be done.

"Stitches hadn't ought to show." Annie Lou was still watching Liza with her bright dark eyes.

Liza groaned. She knew Annie Lou wanted her to take out all the big stitches and start again. Her fingers felt stiff as nails from trying to make the needle move carefully over the cloth. There were pins as well as needles in her feet. They were twisted around the rungs of her chair to help her sit quietly.

"Hate sewing patches," said Liza. But she was careful to speak in a whisper. She began to take out her long, uneven stitches, punching at the cloth to punish it for keeping her inside on such a morning.

It was the day after her visit to the Tillotsons. Now as she sat sewing with Annie Lou she tried to comfort herself by remembering how good she had been since her talk with Mrs. Tillotson. She hadn't liked having Mrs. Tillotson remind her of her duty to her father and the house. But deep inside herself Liza knew that Mrs. Tillotson had been right in all she said.

She had thought about it as she and Seth walked home along the mountain trail. She thought about the warm comfort of the Tillotson kitchen. It was an untidy room, but it was bright with cheerfulness.

She remembered the kitchen at home. It was untidy too, but it wasn't a comfortable untidiness. It looked uncared-for and unloved and it was cold in spite of the fire on the hearth.

The moment she reached home Liza had set to work in a fury of activity. She wanted to make the kitchen look the way her father liked it before he came home. Annie Lou, dozing by the fire, had wakened in a fright at the noise Liza made while she swept and redded the room. Seth had been so alarmed at her energy that he had retired to his corner and pulled a chair in front of himself for protection. It was a tall ladder-back chair and Seth had peered out between the slats, sucking his thumb and watching Liza with round-eyed astonishment. He said nothing. Neither did Annie Lou. Liza made too much noise for conversation.

She swept the floor with such ferocity that the dust rose in a cloud about the room. It made Seth sneeze and set Annie Lou coughing. Liza pretended not to notice. It was only when she started to whisk the sweepings out the door that Annie Lou spoke.

"Hit's borrowin' trouble to sweep out a door," said Annie Lou. She began to rock, moaning to herself.

Liza had no time to argue about trouble. She waited until Annie Lou was looking the other way and swept the dust under the rag carpet. It was out of the way. No one could see it.

Next she attacked the dirty dishes. The noise she made as she clattered the tin plates together and dumped them into the pan of suds was deafening. It drowned Annie Lou's moans and the small whimperings from Seth's corner.

Liza paid no attention. She was up to her elbows in the dishpan and there was water on the table, on the floor and all down the front of her dress. It took her four minutes to do the dishes. She let them dry by themselves while she bundled Seth's laundry into a pile and stuffed it inside the old wardrobe that stood opposite the hearth.

"I'll wash clothes tomorrow," she told herself and shut the door of the wardrobe.

Then Liza stood back to admire her work. The floor was swept, the dishes clean and Seth's laundry was out of sight. "There!" she said and gave a long sigh of satisfaction.

"Lord a-mercy!" said Annie Lou.

Seth crawled out from behind the chair and went straight to the rag carpet. He leaned down to lift it.

"Unna wug," he said and pointed.

"Be quiet," said Liza and snatched him away.

The following morning some of Liza's good intentions stayed with her. She washed the breakfast dishes without being told and decided that the floor didn't need sweeping so soon again. She forgot about Seth's laundry. When Annie Lou reminded her that this was a sewing day, she got out her work with only a few sighs for the brightness of the day outside. But now Liza had been sewing patches for one whole hour and every muscle in her body ached with the agony of sitting still.

"Whar's Seth?" asked Annie Lou as Liza picked wearily at her too-big stitches.

"Out playing," said Liza. She straightened up suddenly. "Reckon I better go see if he's safe."

"Never mind. Adam's outside," said Annie Lou. "I heared your pa tell him to red up the yard."

Liza sat back, her shoulders drooping. There was sun in the yard and a high wind blowing clouds across the sky. She thought of Adam working in the clear brisk air and Seth playing in the dirt nearby. They were boys. They didn't have to sit in a stuffy kitchen and sew patches.

"It's nicer in the sun," she muttered.

She hadn't meant Annie Lou to hear her. But the old woman stopped rocking and peered sharply at Liza.

"Too much sun," said Annie Lou and shook her head. "Too much fine weather fer the time of year. Weather's breedin' trouble."

Liza sniffed.

"Watch and see!" Annie Lou's voice grew shrill. She began to rock again in a fast, jerky motion. "Never no good come of long days of sun."

Liza looked at her. Annie Lou was getting queer, the way she did when she was upset and worried.

"Year of the tide," said Annie Lou suddenly. "High on the hills and sweepin' away . . ." She stopped and hugged her arms across her chest.

"There's no tide," said Liza. "There's been no rain to raise the creek." She wished Adam would come in. Sometimes he could bring Annie Lou back to her senses by talking to her in his calm, even way.

"Her spirit's watchin'," said Annie Lou. She pointed straight at Liza. "She's sent a message."

Liza stood up and threw her sewing on the floor. She couldn't sit still with Annie Lou talking this way. No matter how many times she had heard Annie Lou say these same things in the past few months, Liza could not listen when she talked about her mother's spirit. Annie Lou made it seem as though her mother were right in the room, listening and watching.

"I'm going out," said Liza and ran for the door. Annie Lou called after her, her voice shrill with warning. But Liza paid no heed. She was outside at last, out in the free-blowing air and sun. She saw Adam in the garden patch, clearing the ground for the plowing. Seth was with him, trudging along behind, trying to help.

"Adam!"

It was a relief just to shout.

Adam waved at her and Seth gave a welcoming cry. Liza ran toward them, leaping as she ran. The wind blew away the last stuffy memory of the kitchen.

"Where's Father?" she asked when she reached the spot where Adam was working. She reached down and gave Seth a hard hug just to show she knew he was there.

"Hunting," said Adam shortly. He tugged at a stubborn turnip root.

"Why didn't you go?" asked Liza. She was watching a high, scudding cloud, not thinking what she said.

She remembered when Adam answered her. He reminded her that he had taken his rifle to the blacksmith's the afternoon before to have the broken stock mended.

"Said he could have it ready later on this day," said Adam.

Liza's face grew hot with mortification.

"Did Father say you had to spend out of your savings for the rifle?" she asked, not daring to look at him. She knew that Adam was saving money, bit by tiny bit, to get enough to order a book from the Wish Book. It was a dictionary book he wanted and he had been saving for it for a long time because it cost almost four whole dollars.

Adam shrugged without looking at her and Liza knew she had guessed right. She didn't know what to say. She thought of the tin bank in her chest of drawers. It was empty. Liza scraped her toe along the furrow near her feet.

"If Father sold the trees we'd have cash money to buy the dictionary book," she said at last. "We could get a lot of books and . . . and . . ." She stopped because she had almost mentioned the jeans and this was no time to talk about them.

Adam gave her a swift look. She saw the sudden light in his eyes and she saw it fade away the next moment. "Don't talk so," he said. "He's set against selling." He pulled at another dead stalk. "And so am I," he added but his voice was not as firm as before.

"Don't see the harm of selling trees," said Liza, who was now fired with the idea of having money for Adam's book. "I saw a man from the Lumber Company yesterday and he was real nice. I could ask him if . . ."

"Don't think on it, Liza," said Adam impatiently. "It's not for girls to clutter their heads with such things and don't go talking to any Lumber Company men."

Liza's bright hopes crashed. She didn't like to have Adam tell her that she had no rightful part in important matters. She frowned at his back. He was as bad as the others. No one sympathized with her.

"Verm!"

Seth's joyful cry roused her and she turned to see him bent double over a hole he had scratched in the soft earth. One fat finger jabbed at a large worm which was making a wriggling effort to escape his attentions.

Liza helped extract the worm and soon forgot the unhappy fact that she was only a girl in grubbing up more worms for Seth.

"Feeda chicks," said Seth when he had a handful of them.

Liza let him go to the chicken shed alone. In the past few minutes she had begun to think that she had no right to be angry with Adam. He had been good to her in not letting her get the blame for the broken rifle. He hadn't even complained about spending his dictionary money to have it fixed.

"Adam." Liza waited until he came near as he worked his way along the furrow. "I'm real sorry about the dictionary money."

Adam grinned at her. "Don't fret on it. I can save more."

"I'll help," said Liza eagerly. "I can sew patches and sell quilts like Mother used to do. She got cash money for quilts."

Adam nodded. "Recollect how she ordered the green-leaved paper for the walls with the cash money? Ours is the only cabin in the hollow with real paper on the walls." He spoke proudly.

"It's pretty," said Liza, thinking of the vine-patterned walls of the kitchen. Then she remembered that some of the paper had begun to come away from the walls in the past year. "But it's tearing," she said sadly.

"It could be pasted back," said Adam. "You could do that. It's woman's work."

Liza stared at him. She had never thought that

she would be allowed to mend the green-leaved paper. "I . . . I . . ." she began.

The click of the yard gate interrupted her. Liza saw her father going toward the cabin with a pair of limp rabbits over his shoulder. She and Adam started forward to meet him, but a shout from the creek path beyond the gate stopped them. The voice that hailed Dan Mather was not a friendly one. It was loud with threatening and hard with purpose. Liza and Adam stood still and watched their father.

Dan Mather turned and waited. Three heads appeared at the top of the creek path. The heads became shoulders and then the full height of the neighbor men. They stood with the gate between them and Dan Mather.

Liza had never seen Mr. Tillotson look so grim. All the pleasant lines of his face were drawn together into a disagreeable frown. Mr. Bedford and Mr. Lasher stood back and frowned too. For a long minute no one spoke.

Then Mr. Bedford gave Mr. Tillotson an encouraging push. "You tell him, Sam. Tell him plain."

Mr. Tillotson cleared his throat and began. "We come to talk terms, Dan Mather."

Adam drew in his breath. But he didn't move. Neither did Liza. They watched their father's stiff back and the way his free hand clenched at his side.

But his voice when he spoke was smooth and quiet.

"It's no use, Sam Tillotson. My mind is made up." Each word was a clear and separate sound. It was the way he talked when he was trying to keep his feelings to himself.

"The Lumber Company is waitin' for all of us to say the word." Mr. Tillotson leaned forward over the gate and looked hard at Dan Mather. "I'm givin' mine, so is the others. We want yours."

"You've had it," said Dan Mather. "It's no." He turned his back and went on toward the cabin.

Mr. Tillotson's fist pounded the gate post. "Think what you say, Dan Mather. Think on the cash money."

"Hit's his wife what's holdin' him back. He's tied to her apron strings." Mr. Bedford spoke in a taunting shout, but he stayed well behind Mr. Tillotson.

Liza saw her father turn swiftly, his face white with anger. The next instant he raised his rifle and aimed it straight toward the gate. "Git!" he cried hoarsely. "Git while you can and never come back."

"Father!" Liza's shriek rang into the air. "Don't shoot!"

Her warning was unnecessary. The three men disappeared below the bank like rabbits down a hole. But Mr. Tillotson's voice came from the safety of the creek path in a last angry shout.

"You'll be sorry for this day, Dan Mather!"

"Let none of you set foot on this land again," said Dan Mather in a loud voice. "Him from the Lumber Company can take warning too. I'm shooting."

There was no answer from below the bank. The neighbor men were gone at last.

"Father," said Adam gently. He went toward the cabin and stood by his father's side.

Liza came timidly after him, her eyes on her father's face. She had never seen him look so pale and set.

"There's trouble coming," said Dan Mather heavily. He lowered his rifle and looked from Adam to Liza with eyes that did not seem to know them.

"Father," said Adam again. He reached out to take the rifle, but Dan Mather lifted it suddenly and shook it at the sky.

"Let them come!" he shouted. "Let them try to cut my trees!"

Liza shuddered. Her father sounded almost like Annie Lou with his wild words. Then Adam put his hand on his father's arm and led him toward the cabin. Adam could calm him just as he could soothe Annie Lou when she was wandering in her mind. Dan Mather went willingly, but he held his rifle in his hand.

"Mr. Mather!"

Liza whirled toward the yard gate. The stranger stood there, the man who had been kind to her when she and Seth fell in the creek. She put out her hand in an instinctive warning gesture.

"Hello!" The stranger recognized her and smiled.

"Don't! Oh, don't!"

But Liza was only whispering. The man did not hear. He called to Mr. Mather again and Liza saw her father turn toward the gate, his fingers tightening on his rifle.

Chapter 6

"It's a matter of importance to you, Mr. Mather."

The stranger had opened the gate and stepped into the yard. He paid no attention to the motion of Liza's hands that was meant to keep him away. He was looking toward the porch where Dan Mather stood. Adam was beside him, his face tight with fear.

"You shouldn't . . . he's not . . ." Liza tried to find words to make it clear that the stranger was not welcome. He ought to see for himself that her father was in no mood for company.

But the newcomer only nodded at Liza and took another step forward.

"I'm talking to no man!" The wildness was gone from Dan Mather's voice. He spoke clearly and forcefully.

"I don't believe you understand, Mr. Mather,"

said the stranger quietly. "My name is Barton, Travis Barton, and I've come to . . ."

"You heard me!" said Dan Mather. He lifted his rifle higher, its barrel on a line with the man's shoulders.

Adam moved closer to his father, his hand half-raised toward the rifle.

"You had best git," said Liza quietly.

Mr. Barton looked at her, his eyebrows raised.

"But I only want to . . ." He got no further, for a shrill cry interrupted him. Annie Lou had come out on the porch. She was not bent and huddled now. She stood erect, small and dark in her black dress, her head covered with the old woolen shawl.

"Hit's the message!" cried Annie Lou. She lifted her hands in a wild, free gesture. "Hit's her spirit come back with the message!"

Adam jumped forward and put his arms around Annie Lou. "Hush now," he said. "It's not so."

"Mrs. Mather? Are you Mrs. Mather?" Mr. Barton had a strong voice and his question rang out clear and loud.

"Hit's her! Hit's her!" Annie Lou covered her face with her shawl.

Dan Mather leaped from the porch in one long bound. "Git!" he shouted. "Git from here and don't come back. I'm having no truck with strangers come to ruin the land." He lifted his rifle and took aim.

79

Mr. Barton stood still and stared from Annie Lou to Dan Mather as though he couldn't believe what he saw and heard. He seemed too astonished to move.

But Liza could move. She hurled herself against him, throwing him off balance and out of line with the rifle.

"Git like he says," she cried. "Please, oh please!"

Mr. Barton needed no further urging. In one minute he was outside the gate and halfway down the path to the creek. Liza ran to the rail fence and hung over it.

"It's not . . . I wish . . ." She stopped. There was no way to explain her father's anger or Annie Lou's wild thoughts. She just shook her head.

"You don't understand," said Mr. Barton. He smiled rather shakily at Liza.

"I reckon not," said Liza sadly.

"Liza!"

Her father was calling and Liza knew she must obey him. She waved to Mr. Barton and turned back to the cabin. Annie Lou was gone from the doorway, but her father with Adam beside him waited on the porch.

Liza's feet dragged slowly through the dry dust of the yard. She dreaded the things her father would say to her.

"Liza."

She looked up when Adam spoke. He had come

forward to stand between his father and Liza. "Fetch Seth," he said. "It's time for dinner."

If Dan Mather had wanted to scold her he had no time for it now. Liza was around the corner of the cabin almost before Adam finished speaking. Once out of sight she stopped running and leaned against the clothes post by the back door.

"Whew!"

Liza let out her breath in a long sigh. Adam had saved her once again. "I'll do something for him some day, just you wait and see," she told herself. "I'll think of something to . . ."

A flurry of squawks from the chicken shed brought her thoughts of helping Adam to a halt. She remembered that she was to fetch Seth and the last time she had seen him he had been on his way to the chickens with a gift of worms. The commotion in the shed was a sure sign that Seth, the chickens, or the worms were in trouble. Liza ran to the rescue.

She found Seth seated on the floor of the shed with a bevy of angry, fighting hens clustered about him. Each of the hens wanted the worms that Seth held in his hands and all of them were willing to argue their claims. The dust and feathers rose in a cloud above Seth's head, but he clutched firmly at his worms, shouting manfully above the squawking tumult.

"Taka turn! 'Top peckin'!"

Liza scattered the hens with a sweep of her arms and scooped Seth from the floor. "Look at you! You're a mess." She shook him out, raising another, smaller cloud of dust and feathers. "Give 'em those worms! Chickens don't take turns." She forced open his hands and let the mangled worms drop among the hens.

Seth opened his mouth to protest, but the clucking greed of the hens drowned his cries. Liza escaped from the shed with Seth in her arms.

"Go get your dinner," she told him after she had given his bottom a brisk dusting. "Annie Lou's got it waiting."

"Wiza too," said Seth, pulling at her hand.

"Later," said Liza. "I've got to see Tilda."

It was the best excuse she could think of at the moment for not facing her father. She sent Seth off with another dusty blow at the seat of his overalls and opened the door of the pig's shack.

It was dark inside and the air was heavy with Tilda's personality, but Liza didn't mind. She was used to Tilda's aroma and the gloom and stuffiness of her private domain.

"Here, pig, pig, pig!"

A huge shadow in the corner moved and snuffled.

"Come on, lazy!" Liza prodded at Tilda's bristly bulk. "Come on out in your pen. You need fresh air." She pushed at Tilda until the great pig was on her feet and moving reluctantly toward the runway that led to the pen.

Liza followed her through the low doorway and once in the open air took a long refreshing breath. "Tilda, you're dirty and you smell," she said affectionately.

"Wumph," said Tilda and lay down on her side in an oozing patch of mud. She stretched out her legs and closed her eyes in deep contentment.

Liza perched on Tilda's broad stomach and began to scratch her ears.

"Nothing's going right," said Liza. "Father's cross as sticks and Annie Lou's taking on."

"Hmmm," said Tilda sympathetically.

"Wish he hadn't acted so to that nice man," said Liza. "Seems like there's been a mistake made somehow. He's not at all like that other Lumber man Adam and me saw up at the clearing."

She thought of Mr. Barton's way of smiling so that his eyes smiled too. His voice was quiet and kind. The man she and Adam had seen in the clearing had a harsh, hard voice and he hadn't smiled once. Liza let her shoulders droop forward and her hand fell away from Tilda's ears.

"Grumph?" Tilda opened one eye and looked at Liza.

But Liza was tired of sitting still on Tilda's soft side. She gave the pig a quick pat and jumped to her feet.

As she climbed the side of the pen she remembered another worry. Mr. Tillotson was good and mad at her father now. He'd probably never let her see Emmy again.

As she crossed the garden patch she kicked at a turnip root to relieve her feelings. "Ow!" Her bare toe was no match for the tough old turnip root. "Everything sure is mean," she cried, as she hopped up and down on one foot, rubbing her injured toe. "Wisht I was dead."

"Liza!"

It was Adam calling to her from the back door. Instantly Liza forgot the charms of being dead and ran toward him.

"How is he?" she asked anxiously. "Bad?"

Adam nodded. "He's real overset with folks bothering him to sell. Best to leave him alone. Here." He held a thick slice of bread toward her. "Except for heated-over mush, this is dinner. Eat it."

Liza was only too glad to escape from her father's dark mood and Annie Lou's dinner. She ate the bread in quick gulps.

"Where are you going?" she asked. She guessed that he was going somewhere, for he wore his plaid wool jacket. He also had on his best jeans and shoes. "Going to the Crossings to fetch your rifle, I bet," she said eagerly. "Let me come!" She swallowed the last bit of bread and gave her skirt a hasty brush. "I'm ready."

Adam smiled. "Got your jeans on too?" he asked teasingly.

"Certain sure!" Liza flicked up the edge of her skirt to prove it.

Adam had to laugh. "You're a caution, Liza. You'll never make a home-tending woman with your ways."

The corners of Liza's mouth went down and she looked unhappily at Adam. "I'll act real quiet and polite if you let me come," she said. "Please. Annie Lou can mind Seth for this while. If we go now we'll be back afore the edge of dark."

"Reckon it won't matter," said Adam. "Seth's sleeping now and . . ." He didn't finish, for Liza threw herself at him and hugged him in frantic gratitude.

"Let's hurry," she said. "If Father sees me maybe he'll not like my going." She pulled Adam toward the yard gate.

"No need to hurry so," said Adam as Liza urged him down the bank to the creek path. "Father's shut himself off in his room. He won't see you."

But Liza's gloomy fears were gone now in the rush of the water in the creek and the high wind in the trees. She didn't want to think about her father's unhappiness, Annie Lou's wandering words, or the fact that Seth might need her before she reached home again. She ran ahead of Adam, skipping over the rough spots in the path and dancing on the smooth places. The wind caught at her skirt and tossed the braids on her shoulders. Flecks of sunlight came through the branches above her and danced beside her on the path. Liza shouted aloud with the joy of being Liza.

"It's four miles to the Crossings," said Adam, who came behind her at a slower pace. "You'll be plumb tuckered out before you get there, the way you're going."

"I will not!" shouted Liza. She jumped up on a rock beside the creek and stood there with her arms flung out for balance. There were rocks and stones of all shapes and sizes in the creek bed. They made a scattered pathway through the water. "Race you to the bend on the stones!" she cried. "Get off your shoes, Adam!"

He hesitated, but only for a moment. Adam was not so old and sober-sided that he could resist a challenge like this. By the time he had taken off his shoes and tied them by their laces around his neck, Liza had tucked her skirt into her jeans and was far ahead of him down the creek. She was light and quick. It was no trouble for her to leap and balance from rock to stone. Adam came after her, but he moved more carefully. When the bend was in sight, Liza was still in the lead.

"I beat, I beat!" Liza waved triumphantly at Adam.

"Look out!" he shouted.

But he was too late. Liza lost her balance and was in the creek up to her knees. "Ow!" she wailed as the chill of the water caught her.

"It doesn't do to count chickens before they're hatched," said Adam as he jumped for the rock beyond her. "I beat!" He laughed as Liza waded to the path with water dripping from her jeans.

"Pooh!" Liza made a face at him. "I *almost* beat, anyhow." She wrung the water from her jeans and rubbed furiously at her numbed legs. "I'll warm up if I run," she said and started along the path at a brisk pace.

Once again she was far ahead of Adam, racing over the ground like a leaf before the wind. By the time she came in sight of the cluster of cottonwoods where the creek joined the river, she was out of breath and thoroughly warm.

"Best to rest a bit," said Adam when he joined her. "You're not a fit sight for the Crossings."

"No one to see me but old Mr. Jason," said Liza. She looked toward the cottonwoods where a corner of a roof and a thin wisp of smoke above it proved that the settlement was among the trees. But she tried to smooth her hair with her fingers, tucking the stray ends behind her ears.

"Pull out your skirt," said Adam, who was get-

87

ting his shoes on. "You hadn't ought to come without shoes."

Liza didn't want to argue about shoes now. She pulled her skirt into place and hoped Adam wouldn't mention the wrinkles. "Can I come see the forge?" she asked as they walked at a more sedate pace toward the cottonwoods.

Adam shook his head. "It's no place for girls. I just hope Tom's got my rifle ready. We may be needing it soon."

"Would you shoot, too, if anyone comes on the land?" she asked.

Adam only shrugged his shoulders and Liza forgot her question as they came in sight of the two buildings that made up the Crossings settlement. Liza seldom came to the Crossings. It was too far from home for easy visiting. Sometimes months would go by before she left the Middle Folds and came down to this one settled place in the Hundredfold Hills. There was little to see and nothing to do here, but to Liza it was an adventure to come to the Crossings.

Blacksmith Tom's shop was a small rickety building set beneath a giant cottonwood as though it hoped for support from its huge trunk. Smoke rose from the tin chimney and a sound of hammering came from inside.

Liza stood on the path and peered into the dark depths of the shop. She saw a red glow and the shadow of a lifting arm. She looked hopefully at Adam. It would be fun to know the reason for those sounds and to warm herself in the heat of the fire.

But Adam shook his head and pointed to the building opposite. This was Mr. Jason's place of business, larger but even more ramshackle than the blacksmith's. Mr. Jason kept a store that sold sugar and canned goods; he was the postmaster, too, and he traded anything the hill people brought to him for cash money or for goods.

Liza needed no urging to visit Mr. Jason's store. Before Adam could reach the blacksmith's door she had skipped across the dusty road and was inside the store. Mr. Jason, a small, whiskery man with a face like a withered butternut and sharp, darting eyes, greeted her from behind his laden counter.

"Come down outa the holler, eh?" He laughed, a queer cracked laugh that always reminded Liza of a hen cackling.

"Yes," said Liza. She didn't want to waste time talking. There was too much to see and wish for on the shelves and counter. Her eyes went from the rows of canned goods with their bright labels to the heaps of work clothes, the real leather shoes, and the packets of garden seeds. She wanted them all, even the work clothes, for a pair of boy's jeans caught her attention immediately. Liza looked

quickly away from the jeans and fixed her eyes on the sugar barrel. It would never do to let Mr. Jason know that she was interested in boy's pants.

"Got some pieces of mail fer ye," said Mr. Jason, who didn't mind carrying on the conversation by himself. He rummaged in a drawer beneath the counter and found a slim package of envelopes. "Nothin' but throw-away mail," he said and tossed the bundle at Liza. "Jist them advertisements and printed stuff. You folks ain't been gettin' no real mail since yore ma passed. Ain't sent any letters up creek fer a long spell now."

Liza nodded. She wasn't listening. The Mather family seldom got letters. She never looked for a messenger from Mr. Jason, who delivered the mail by giving it to anyone going the same way as the letter.

"Times sure change," said Mr. Jason as Liza gazed at the row of candy jars above his head. There were peppermints, horehound drops, and licorice in those jars. Liza's mouth watered but she made herself look away from them. She had no money for candy. She fixed her attention on the piles of dress goods near the door.

"Sam Tillotson was in yesterday," said Mr. Jason. "He's real riled at yore pa. Never seen Sam take on so afore."

This was not a subject that Liza wanted to talk about. She moved slowly toward the door, her eyes still searching the shelves hungrily. She wanted to be able to remember all she had seen. It would be something to think about when she was in bed at night.

"Folks over to the next holler bin orderin' right smart from the Wish Book," said Mr. Jason. "Buyin' goods off me too. The Lumber Company paid cash money for them trees of theirs. Maybe you oughta tell yore pa how they . . ."

But Liza was outside the door now. Mr. Jason's cackling laugh came after her. "Looks like there's trouble brewin' if yore pa holds out," cried Mr. Jason. "He might better think on sellin'."

Liza didn't want to hear about the people who had cash money to spend or about any trouble that might come. She glanced at the envelopes in her hand. As Mr. Jason had said, they were all advertisements. There was nothing in any of them that Liza could buy and she tossed them into the weeds beneath Mr. Jason's tilted porch.

"Liza, come quick!"

Adam called from across the road and Liza turned swiftly toward him. She didn't need to see his face to know that something was wrong. His tight, hard voice told her that. She saw his rifle in his hand, mended and ready for use. He gestured with it, motioning her to hurry.

"We've got to get back," he said as she ran forward. "We've got to get back to the land right quick."

Chapter 7

"Remember! Act natural as if nothing was wrong."

Liza nodded. There was a thousand explanations she wanted from Adam. All the long miles from the Crossings she had followed at his heels, asking questions, begging to know what he had heard at Blacksmith Tom's that had so upset him.

But Adam had only shaken his head as though to rid himself of a swarm of mosquitoes. He had hurried on ahead of her, his eyes fixed on the path. Liza could see his fingers clutched bone-white around his rifle.

Liza had skipped and run to keep up with his long strides. Sometimes she had stopped to catch her breath. But she had always run on again, keeping as near Adam as she could.

When they came in sight of the great beech tree

that marked the edge of the Mather property, Adam had stopped to wait for her.

"Father mustn't hear," he said.

"Hear what?" demanded Liza. "Tell me what you heard."

Adam didn't answer, but at the yard gate he repeated his warning.

"Can't act natural if I don't feel natural," said Liza. "Something real bad happened and now you won't tell me."

"Later," said Adam and went on toward the cabin.

Seth was in his chair at the table when they came in the door. He greeted Liza with a shout and held out his arms to her. As she hugged him, Liza looked over his shoulder toward her father's door. It was still shut fast.

"Supper's waitin'," said Annie Lou from her rocker. Her bright, quick eyes went from Adam's drawn face to Liza's worried frown. "Yore pa's shut hisself off," she added unnecessarily. The rocker began to move back and forth, rustling and creaking in tune with Annie Lou's uneasiness.

"He's resting," said Adam.

Liza knew from the way he spoke that he didn't want Annie Lou to start seeing things and wandering in her mind. He nodded toward the fireplace as a signal that she was to stir up the fire and get the supper on the table.

"It's mush again," said Liza when she took the lid off the pot. "Mush and bacon." She poked at the few pieces of greasy bacon in the skillet. "Seems as if we've been eating nothing else since . . ."

"Never mind!"

Adam spoke so sharply that Liza looked at him, her eyebrows raised. He was sitting near Seth, his elbows on the table and his chin in his hands. His rifle rested against his chair. Liza knew that he hadn't meant to be cross with her. He only wanted peace and quiet so he could think.

Liza hurried with the supper. She stirred up the mush and heated the bacon in record time. As she put the tin plate in front of Adam she nudged his arm and gestured toward her father's door.

Adam shook his head. "Best to leave him be," he muttered.

He began to eat before Liza brought her own plate to the table. With their father absent, there was no thought of saying grace. They ate in silence.

The only sound in the room was the unhappy crooning from Annie Lou's corner and the scrape of spoons on the tin plates. Seth had already eaten and had fallen asleep with his head resting on the edge of the table. A small river of milk and mush ran off the table where he had upset his bowl. But Liza was too busy watching Adam to worry about spilt milk.

"She oughta get along home," said Annie Lou

suddenly. Her voice was clear and high and Liza dropped her spoon with a clatter. She knew Annie Lou was talking about her mother.

"I'll get Seth to bed," she said loudly. If she talked about ordinary things perhaps Annie Lou would come around to sensible thinking. She bundled Seth hurriedly into her arms and wakened him to a wail of complaint.

"Hush now, hush," she said. She put her hand over his mouth and looked nervously toward her father's door.

But Seth would not be comforted. He began to kick at the table. His bowl rolled and crashed to the floor. Annie Lou's voice rose with the misery of her feelings. The room rang with sound and Adam put his hands over his ears.

Liza heard the squeak of her father's door as she struggled to get a hold on Seth's furious feet. She saw him standing in the doorway and searched his face with quick concern. He looked just as he had when she last saw him except for one thing. His eyes were not dark with anger now. There was a small twinkling light in them as he watched her efforts to calm Seth.

"Give him here," said Dan Mather and held out his arms.

Liza's heart took a swift upward leap. "Here he is and welcome," she said.

Dan Mather sat down at the table with Seth on

his lap. "Hush your noise," he said and Seth was quiet.

Liza looked gratefully at her father. When he was this way, calm and kind-spoken, the whole room was lighter and warmer. Even Annie Lou seemed to feel the difference in the room. She stopped rocking and she wasn't moaning any more.

"Was the rifle ready?" asked Dan Mather.

"Fixed good as new," said Adam.

Liza knew from the way he spoke that he was trying to sound easy in his talk.

"I went to the store," said Liza, who was anxious to get the conversation onto a safe subject. "Mr. Jason says the folks in the next hollow are buying up . . ." She stopped, her face reddening at the nearness of what she had almost said. "There's seeds at the store," she said loudly.

" 'Most time for planting," said Dan Mather. "Season's right early this year."

"Weather's breedin' trouble," said Annie Lou. She spoke as though she were merely mentioning a sensible fact.

"We can begin the plowing any day now," said Dan Mather, nodding at Adam.

"Teth too," said Seth. But he didn't say it very loud. He was almost asleep again, safe and comfortable in his father's arms.

Liza prepared her father's dinner, heaping the plate with the least lumpy remains of the mush and heating the bacon to a crispy brown. He smiled at her as she set the plate before him, but sighed when he saw the familiar mush.

"We can have stew tomorrow," said Liza quickly as she remembered the rabbits he had brought home that morning. "I'll make it," she added and wondered for a fleeting second if she knew how. But she brushed the doubt aside. Annie Lou could make it if she couldn't.

"Take Seth," said Dan Mather as he prepared to eat. "He's sleeping quiet."

Liza hurried getting Seth to bed. She didn't bother to take off his clothes. It was no use to rouse him. She looked at his grimy hands and the traces of mush on his round cheeks. She covered them quickly with his quilt.

"I'll wash him tomorrow," she thought, and went back to the kitchen.

Her father was talking when Liza sat down at the table. He was speaking of the troubles of the morning, but he was not angry now. "Sam and the rest are all stirred up with the talk of cash money," he said easily. "They'll forget it when the Lumber folk leave the Hundredfold."

Adam shook his head but so slightly that only Liza noticed.

"Thinking of cash money brings out the worst in some folks," said Dan Mather. "It gets 'em thinking mean thoughts." He wiped his plate clean with a piece of bread and sat back from the table. "The trees are more to me than cash money," he said. Then he added in a voice that was almost a whisper, "They meant the same to her."

Liza stared at the table top. Her father seldom mentioned her mother, except when he said grace. He kept his sorrow locked inside him and it only showed in his silent ways. When he roused himself to be friendly as he had during supper, Liza knew he wanted to show his family that he thought of them.

"I don't hold with selling," said Adam.

"Me neither," said Liza quickly.

"That's a comfort to me," said Dan Mather. He got up from his chair and stretched his arms high over his head. "Time for sleeping if we start plowing tomorrow. Rest well."

He went back to his room and once again the door closed behind him.

"His spirit's sore uneasy," said Annie Lou. She pulled her shawl about her, tucking an assortment of bits and pieces of her hidden treasure into its folds as she always did before she went to bed.

Liza didn't answer Annie Lou and Adam was too far away in his own thoughts to heed. But Liza was determined to make him share these thoughts with her once they were alone. She watched impatiently as Annie Lou gathered herself and her possessions together. It seemed an age before the last tiny packet was folded into her shawl or arranged in its proper place in the old chair.

"Good night and rest well," said Liza as Annie Lou made a motion to rise.

"Hain't gone yet," said Annie Lou. She shifted a knobby bundle of piecework from one corner of the chair to another.

Liza groaned aloud. But nothing hurried Annie Lou. It was a good five minutes before she finished her night settling and shuffled off to her room. She gave Liza a queer little smile as she went past the table and Liza suspected that Annie Lou had been slow on purpose to fret her.

"Can't tell when she's right in the head or not," said Liza when she and Adam were at last alone.

"She doesn't miss much," said Adam. There was a teasing note in his voice that made Liza realize he knew exactly why she wanted to be alone with him.

"What happened at the Crossings?" asked Liza, taking quick advantage of his lightened mood.

Adam's face clouded. "It's them," he said at last. "They're planning trouble, bad trouble." He spoke so quietly that his words scarcely came across the table to Liza. But they were plain enough to make her stiffen. She knew Adam was talking about Sam Tillotson and the other neighbors in the hollow. But even her lively imagination could not tell her what the "bad trouble" was.

"Wh—— wh——." The word stuck in her throat.

Adam looked straight at her, his eyes narrow and strangely bright. "Blasting sticks," he said, his voice hard and even. "Sam Tillotson bought some off Tom this morning. He told me so."

"Blasting sticks!" Liza's hands grew cold. She remembered the few times she had heard the heavy thunder of dynamiting in the hills. It was deeper and darker than any thunder from the sky. ....

"Sam made out he had some rock to blast on his land," said Adam. "But I don't believe it." He got suddenly to his feet. "Sam's too lazy to take trouble with his land. He and the others are planning something and I've got to stop it."

"How?" Liza was standing now. "Stop what?"

Adam shifted his rifle from one hand to the other. "I don't know for sure," he said grimly. "I've got to find out and I've got to keep a watch on the land."

There was something in the way he spoke that made Liza think that he hadn't told her all he knew. Her curiosity flamed to a new pitch. "What are you going to do?" she demanded.

"Keep a watch on the land like I said," said Adam impatiently. "If they mean harm it's at night they'll do harm. Listen now!" He leaned toward her. "Father mustn't know what I heard. There's no knowing what he might do in his anger if he hears Sam has been buying up blasting sticks. You hear me?"

Liza nodded. She was too impressed by Adam's words to speak.

"I wouldn't tell you except you have to know in case Father wakes and finds me gone," said Adam. "Then you must say I'm off hunting."

"Father won't wake once he's asleep," said Liza. "Let me come too. I could help and . . ."

Adam stopped her with a look. "Go to bed," he said shortly. "This is man's work."

Liza knew that Adam meant what he said. She watched him as he went out the door with his rifle in his hand. He did not look back and Liza was left alone in the quiet of the kitchen. The fire had been banked and the room was dim and cold. She shivered.

"Best to go to bed," she said out loud.

Three minutes later Liza was in bed with the quilt pulled up to her chin. She was sure she would never get to sleep. Her mind raced over what Adam had told her. She thought of the blasting sticks but she couldn't imagine what Sam Tillotson meant to do with them. Maybe Adam was wrong. Maybe Sam really was going to blast rocks on his land.

She even thought of the stranger, the man who called himself Travis Barton. He was kind and nice and he had saved Seth and her from the creek.

Maybe he could save them all from the trouble if he only knew about it.

Liza yawned and snuggled closer under her quilt. It was warm and safe in bed. It was hard to think that anyone meant harm when she was so comfortable.

She listened to the sound of Seth's soft breathing. It was like a lullaby. Liza's eyes closed. She was asleep.

"Liza!"

The voice came out of her half-dreams. It was as though someone were calling her, trying to make her listen. Liza drifted deeper into sleep.

"Liza! Hear me!" A rapping sound accompanied the pleading cry.

The words and knocking were real. Liza sat up and listened.

Chapter 8

"TELL it again, Emmy. Tell it real plain."

Liza hung out the window, clutching at the sill with both hands to keep her balance. It was hard to hear Emmy's soft, frightened voice. It was even harder to see her in the pale light of the early morning.

"I said it plain. I can't bide. I got to get back." Emmy's words were thick with tears.

Liza took a deep breath to steady her leaping thoughts. She tried to make herself believe that anything was real about the few moments that had passed since Emmy's voice roused her.

She remembered hearing the voice calling through her dreams and how she had at last known that the voice was real. It had taken her only a minute to reach the window and discover the startling fact that it was morning. Emmy's breathless whisper, coming from the shelter of the bushes by the back door, had been like a voice from nowhere.

"You say your ma sent you?"

Liza tried to sound quiet and easy. Emmy might calm herself if she pretended there was nothing unusual about being here at this unearthly hour of day.

"I told you that." Emmy spoke crossly and her voice rose. She moved from the shadows and crept toward the window.

Liza saw her face, pale and streaked with tears, and her round fearful eyes.

"It's like I said. Ma sent me to tell you there's trouble meant for your family. She don't know what, but she don't like the way Pa is acting. You better be real careful, Ma says, if you . . . What's that?"

Emmy's voice thinned and she crouched closer to the window. Liza heard the footsteps near the front of the house and said hurriedly, "It's only Adam. You don't need to . . ."

But she was talking to empty air. Liza caught a glimpse of a light skirt as it whisked into the black shadow of the trees. Emmy was already on the footpath that led toward home.

"Lord a-mercy!" Liza stared at the place where Emmy had disappeared, wondering for a second if she really had been there and delivered her mother's message. Then she remembered what

Adam had told her the night before and how he had passed the long night on patrol. It was real enough. Adam knew it and so did Mrs. Tillotson. The neighbors were planning trouble.

She heard a sound in the kitchen and realized she ought to tell Adam of Emmy's warning. Liza snatched up her jacket and opened her door carefully.

Adam was leaning over the fire, warming his hands over the banked coals. He looked up as Liza came toward him, his face tense with sudden alarm.

"It's you," he said and the relief was plain in his voice. "What you doing awake so early?"

Liza huddled close to the fire and pulled her jacket closer over her shoulders. The kitchen was cold as a cavern and the pale light from the windows made strange shadows out of the familiar shapes in the room.

"Tisn't so early," she said and shivered. "Emmy's been here."

"What?" Adam stared at her. "What for?"

As Liza repeated Emmy's message she couldn't resist making it sound more dramatic than Emmy's frightened whispers. "She says her pa and the others are bound to do something terrible and her ma's fretted to death and taking on like anything. Emmy was pale like a ghost and crying something awful. What'll they do, Adam? Did you see anything last night?"

Adam shook his head. "Not a sight or sound. I walked all over the land and there was nothing. Emmy's ma sent her, you say?" Adam began pacing the floor.

Liza nodded. There was something in the way Adam moved and talked that made her doubly uneasy.

"Mrs. Tillotson always makes Mr. Tillotson do what she wants," said Liza suddenly. "She ought to stop him."

"Not when he's got his mind set on cash money,"

said Adam. He came toward the fireplace. His rifle was resting against the stonework and his hands closed over it in a fierce grip. "He can't harm us," he said loudly. "Not Sam Tillotson nor any of them."

Liza looked up at him and knew that he meant what he said with every bone and muscle in his body. But Adam's bones were young and his muscles were not as strong as those of a man grown. She wondered if the job of protecting the family might not be too much for him.

"Maybe we ought to tell Father," she said softly.

"Think what you say," said Adam.

Liza remembered how her father had looked the day he threatened Sam Tillotson with his gun. There was no telling what he might do if he knew Sam was really planning trouble.

"Annie Lou's right about one thing," said Adam, rubbing his hands along the muzzle of his rifle. "If Mother were here all this would never be. Somehow she would have made things peaceable and neighborly again."

"I know," said Liza. "I wish I . . ." She stopped. There was no use saying she wished she was like her mother. She knew she wasn't. She did not have her mother's gentle ways and her influence over other people.

But thinking about her mother made Liza realize that her mother would never have sat still in a cold room when there was a hungry man waiting for his breakfast. She threw off her jacket and made a bustle of stoking up the fire and heating the pot.

"Maybe Annie Lou can skin the rabbits today," she said as she put some bacon in the skillet. "I can make a stew."

Adam only nodded. He scarcely seemed to hear Liza or notice what she was doing. He even refused to eat the breakfast that Liza put on the table.

"I can't fetch an appetite," he said, pushing the tin plate away.

"Maybe you better sleep," said Liza, who was making a hearty breakfast of fried bread and bacon. "You don't have to keep watch in the daytime. They won't try anything in the light." She talked with her mouth full, but she tried to sound comfortable and easy for Adam's sake.

"Maybe the trouble won't come in the day," said Adam wearily, "but I've no time for sleep. We begin the plowing today and Father needs help."

Liza didn't argue. There was something impatient in the way Adam spoke that showed her he didn't want to be told what to do. She saw the shadows under his eyes and wished that she had a woman's way of making Adam do what was best for him. He wouldn't eat and he wouldn't rest and there was nothing she could do to make him.

Adam leaned on the table and rested his head on his folded hands. He wasn't sleeping. Liza could tell by the way he held his shoulders that he was awake and waiting for what might come. She finished her breakfast and sat back in her chair, watching Adam.

It was quiet in the room. The fire snapped and crackled on the hearth, but it was the only sound. Liza wanted to be still so as not to disturb Adam, but in five minutes her legs began to twitch. She stretched one foot as far as it would go, then she stretched the other foot. It was no use. Her legs still twitched and ached for action. She sighed, but she was careful to make it a small, soft sigh. It was still early. Seth wouldn't be awake for another hour. Neither would her father or Annie Lou. The hour reached ahead of her in a long space of emptiness.

On the wall behind Adam's head was a hanging shred of the green-leaved wallpaper. Liza stared at it. Then her eyes traveled all around the walls. Tatters and strips hung from a dozen places.

Suddenly Liza leaped to her feet. She had something to do at last.

Adam looked up, but he did not move from his chair or say a word as Liza dragged the flour barrel from its corner. He watched her as she mixed a bowl of flour paste, stirring it to a sticky mess with a wooden spoon.

"There," said Liza, stabbing at the lumps with her spoon. "That'll be enough to paste up that old paper."

"Enough to paper fifty rooms," said Adam.

"Pooh," said Liza. She didn't mind what Adam said as long as he sounded cheerful and teasing again.

In the next hour Liza smeared the flour paste on the torn wallpaper, on her face, and on her arms up to the elbows. The hanging paper was back on the walls, coated with a thick mass of paste.

"It doesn't look right somehow," said Liza, stepping back to study her work. "Will that extra paste come off?

"Wait till it dries," said Adam. "It might rub off."

"Maybe Father won't like it," said Liza doubtfully. She looked at the blotches of drying paste and sighed. All that work—and the paper now looked worse than ever.

"He won't mind," said Adam. "Likely he won't notice."

Liza didn't answer. Now Adam had lost interest in her efforts and probably her father wouldn't notice what she had done. She sighed heavily as she bent over the water bucket and scrubbed at her arms and hands. All her work was for nothing.

A wailing sound from her room announced that Seth was awake and wanting attention. Liza dried her hands hurriedly and wiped the towel over her face.

"Liza."

Liza looked back at Adam from her door.

"It's a good job," he said.

Instantly she felt better. She was warm and comfortable inside now. Even if the walls were smeared and patchy with paste, it didn't matter as long as Adam appreciated her work.

Later when Liza was giving Seth his breakfast she watched her father carefully, waiting to see if he noticed the mended paper. But it was just as Adam had said. Her father was too busy thinking of other things to look at the walls.

"You can hitch up Old Ben," he told Adam as he finished eating. "It's another good day and we can start the plowing."

"Too much sun for the season," said Annie Lou. She was in her chair, getting out her piecework.

No one paid attention to Annie Lou. She said the same thing every time anyone mentioned the good weather. But Liza saw the little squares of cloth Annie Lou was sorting over and made up her mind that this was no day to sew patches.

"Me and Seth can help with the plowing," she said quickly. She stuffed the last bit of breakfast into Seth's mouth and pulled him off his chair. "I can ride Old Ben when you guide the plow."

"Adam's riding," said Dan Mather. "Skirts has no place on a mule's back."

Liza knew enough not to mention the old pants she could wear if she rode Old Ben. The important thing now was to get out of the house before Annie Lou began talking about sewing patches. She waited until her father and Adam left the kitchen, then she took Seth by the hand and went quietly toward the door.

"Where going?" demanded Seth, much too loudly.

Annie Lou looked up. She opened her mouth but the door was open too. Liza was on the porch, dragging Seth after her, before Annie Lou had time to say one word about patches.

"You be quiet," whispered Liza, giving Seth a small shake.

"Quite," said Seth and put his hands over his mouth.

"Stay that way," said Liza. They were off the porch now and safe from Annie Lou. "If we don't get in the way maybe we can help plow even if I can't ride Old Ben." But she knew that it was Adam who would ride the mule all day while her father guided the plow through the furrows. She would be lucky if she were allowed to pick up sticks and litter in the rows behind.

"Better than sewing patches anyhow," she said as she took Seth's hand once more and led him toward the garden.

Liza had guessed right. It was Adam who rode Old Ben all the morning while she and Seth were given the drudging task of picking up after the plow. It was dusty work and she had most of it to do alone, for Seth soon tired of picking up sticks and tossing them down again. He went off to see the chickens.

By noon half the patch was done and Liza was thoroughly tired of dust and litter. It was almost a relief to go in the house and help Annie Lou with the dinner. Annie Lou had made a stew from the two rabbits and, as she helped dish it out, Liza hoped Adam wouldn't remember that she had said she was going to make it herself.

But Adam was not in a mood to notice anything when he and his father came in to eat. He was white with weariness and his hand shook as he pushed his plate away.

"I can't eat," he told Liza in a whisper. He nodded toward the end of the table as a signal that Liza was not to let his father know that he could not eat his dinner. Fortunately Dan Mather was too busy with his own thoughts and food to see that Adam's plate remained untouched.

"You hadn't ought to be riding Old Ben," said Liza when the silent meal was over. She had waited until her father left the room to say what had been in her mind all during dinner.

"It's all right," said Adam. He brushed his hand across his eyes and straightened his shoulders. "I can ride."

"You're wore out and . . ." But Liza got no further. Adam was already following his father toward the garden.

Liza trailed after him, her heart heavy within her. There was a long afternoon of work ahead of Adam and there was no way for her to help him.

That evening Adam ate no supper either. He was bone white now and his eyes burned bright with weariness. He sat at his place with his hands braced against the table. But he sat straight and held his head high. Liza could not look at him. She knew that Adam meant to go out again that night and keep watch on the land.

"He can't, he mustn't," she told herself over and over again. There must be some way to stop him and make him get the rest he needed. Her head churned with all the things she might do to make him bide at home. But she knew at the same time that Adam would not listen to her.

Liza waited all through dinner, through the time it took to wash the dishes, get Seth to bed, and watch Annie Lou's endless fussing over her night settling. There had been little waiting for Dan Mather to leave the kitchen. He had gone to his room as soon as he finished eating.

The moment she and Adam were alone, she caught at his arm and held it fast. "Let me go," she said. "Let me watch the land tonight."

"No," said Adam. It seemed the only word he had strength to say. He took up his rifle, but his fingers scarcely gripped the stock. He pulled away from Liza's hold and stumbled as he went toward the door.

"I'll tell Father!"

Liza's desperate cry forced Adam to a halt. He swung toward her, his hand on the door jamb for support. "You can't," he whispered hoarsely. "You know what he'd do." He swayed away from the door, his knees bent beneath him. "Liza, you . . ."

But Adam had fallen and could not finish what he meant to say.

Chapter 9

"FETCH some herb tea."

These were the first words Dan Mather had spoken since Liza's shrill screaming brought him running to the kitchen. He had said nothing as he lifted Adam in his arms and carried him to his bed. He hadn't asked a single question or told Liza to stop her crying.

Liza's screams had roused Annie Lou, too, and the old woman had come from her room, her shawl clutched about her and her eyes bright with fear. She had stood at the foot of Adam's bed, wailing and rocking on her heels at the sight of his deathlike stillness.

"He's kilt, kilt stone dead," moaned Annie Lou. "Hit's the trouble I seen comin'. Hit's her spirit come to call him."

It was then that Dan Mather had ordered Annie Lou to fetch the herb tea. Annie Lou's herb tea was famous in the Hundredfold. It was strong and it cured the stomach complaint as no other medicine could.

"It's not the complaint," said Liza. "He's plumb empty and wore out." But no one paid attention to her. She crouched by Adam's bed, cold with fear and misery.

Dan Mather got a cloth and wrung it out in the ice-cold water in the bucket. His hands were gentle as a woman's as he wiped Adam's forehead. He talked soothingly, quiet words that had no meaning but had sympathy in their sound.

Liza stayed near the bed. There was nothing for her to do but pray that Adam would open his eyes and show that he was not dead. She knew why he had fallen. He was hungry and tired and his head was filled with worry. But she couldn't tell her father.

"It's what comes of too much night reading," said Dan Mather, as he wrung out the cloth once more in the bucket.

"He wasn't reading," said Liza. "He was . . ." She stopped and pretended to be busy smoothing Adam's pillow. "He's not been reading for two nights."

Her father frowned at her and Liza knew that she was not to argue about the bad effects of night reading. He would do more than frown if he knew what Adam really had been doing the night before. She bent nearer to Adam, searching his face for a sign of life.

"He's moving," she cried. "Adam!" She forgot that she was meant to be quiet and shouted his name.

"Hush you!" said her father sternly.

"But he moved. I saw him," said Liza, who had seen the slight motion of Adam's head on the pillow. "He's alive!"

"Sure am," said Adam. His voice was no more than a breath, but Liza heard it clearly. She flung her arms around him and hugged him in a burst of relief.

This time her father did not try to stop her. He stood near the bed, watching Adam.

"I thank God," said Dan Mather quietly.

Adam's eyes were open now and he looked at the faces near him with a puzzled questioning. Then he frowned and his whole body stiffened. "I must get up," he muttered. "I must go out and . . ."

Liza's fingers closed over his arm in a fierce grip, cutting him off short. He turned to her, his eyes wild and staring. Then he nodded. "I was forgetting," he murmured.

Dan Mather had gone to the fireplace to hurry Annie Lou's making of the herb tea. He did not hear Adam's last words and Liza sighed thankfully.

"You be still," she told Adam, pushing him back on the pillow. "You can't rise."

"I must. I have to . . ." But Adam, who had made one struggle to sit up, could not go on. He was too weak to speak, much less to move.

Liza's heart sank within her. She knew that she must tell Adam that she would take the rifle and guard the land this night. It was the only thing she could do to ease his fears and her own fears must not stop her. She thought of the dark woods, the loneliness of the night, and the unknown trouble that might come. Then she shoved all these things to the back of her mind.

"Don't fret," she whispered so that only he might hear. "I can do the watching. I can for certain sure."

Adam had time to give her only one look before Dan Mather brought the herb tea. Annie Lou trailed after him and leaned over the foot of the bed to peer at Adam.

"The spirits is callin' like I said," muttered Annie Lou. She was like a queer old bird as she crouched over the footboard, her voice thin with her misery.

"Don't take on," said Dan Mather. "There's no cause for fret. Adam needs rest." He handed the cup to Liza and put his arm around Annie Lou's bent shoulders. "Come," he said.

Annie Lou let herself be led to her room. But

just before she reached the door she pulled away from Dan Mather's protecting arm and darted to the fireplace. Adam's rifle was resting against the chimney piece and Annie Lou snatched it up.

"Hit's to ward off the evil spirits," she said and thrust the rifle under Adam's bed. "You'll rest easy now," she told him and shuffled off to her room, plainly much comforted in her mind.

"Leave it be," said Dan Mather. "It can do no harm."

Liza had been so surprised at Annie Lou's sudden energy that she had spilt some of the herb tea over her hand. She had no time to worry over Annie Lou's crazy notions as she rubbed at the burned place and tried to stir the tea at the same time. In any case the rifle was near at hand when she needed it.

"You bide with him a while," said Dan Mather when Adam had finished the tea. "Wake me along about midnight and I'll take my turn to watch."

Liza nodded. She didn't dare think about what she would be doing at midnight. She would be out in the darkness of the hills and she could only hope that her father would not waken by himself and know that she was gone.

When she and Adam were alone there was little that needed saying. Adam lay with his eyes closed, so still that Liza had to hold her own breath to make certain he was still breathing. The tea had done him some good for there were faint patches of color on his cheeks.

"You should eat," said Liza at last.

"Reckon so," said Adam quietly. He turned his head in the direction of her voice. "If I eat, I can get strength to go out and . . ."

"No!" Liza jumped to her feet. "You're not moving this night. Hear me?"

Adam smiled faintly. "Tisn't likely I can fight you about that now," he said. "Fetch me some of the stew and we'll see."

The remains of the rabbit stew were still warm in the hanging pot and Liza heaped a plate for Adam. He was too weak to sit upright to eat so Liza fed him in slow spoonfuls, glad that she could do something to help him.

It was only when he clenched his teeth and refused to open them that Liza knew he would eat no more.

"Like stuffing a goose," said Adam as Liza put the plate away. "You bide a time and I'll be fixed to go out."

"You're not stirring," said Liza. "You're going to . . ." She looked at Adam and stopped.

His eyes were closed once more, but his jaw was set. Liza knew that talk would do no good. Adam was set on going out as soon as he could gather enough strength to move. It was up to her to find a way to stop him.

122

She sat down beside his bed once more and took his hand in hers. He was breathing quietly, almost as though he were asleep. Liza bent forward and began to sing. It was one of the old hill songs that Annie Lou sang so often.

I gave my love a cherry that had no stone,
I gave my love a chicken that had no bone,
I gave my love a ring that had no end,
I gave my love a baby with no cryin'.

How can there be a cherry that has no stone?
How can there be a chicken that has no bone?
How can there be a ring that has no end?
How can there be a baby with no cryin'?

A cherry when it's blooming, it has no stone,
A chicken when it's peeping, it has no bone,
A ring when it's rolling, it has no end,
A baby when it's sleeping, has no cryin'.

Liza sang as she sometimes did to Seth, so quietly that the words and the tune were one soft sound. As she finished the second verse she smiled. The tense line along Adam's jaw had softened, he was breathing deeply and slowly. He was asleep. Liza finished the song in a whispering breath.

"Adam."

She said his name as loudly as she dared. He did not move or hear her. Liza tucked his quilt close about him. Then she reached down and took the rifle from under the bed. The steel felt cold on her hands and she shivered. It was cold out on the hills too. But there was no time for fear now.

The wooden clock on the mantel said nine o'clock when Liza opened the door and went quietly outside. She had taken time to change into the old jeans and to tie a scarf over her head. If she were seen on the mountain, she would be taken for a boy, a boy with a gun and therefore someone to reckon with.

"Brr!" It was colder than she had imagined. A brisk, hurrying wind tossed the branches of the trees above the creek and sent a pack of rolling clouds across the sky. There were stars in the sky, too, and a moon, rising over the hill behind the cabin. It wouldn't be black dark with the moon and the stars and Liza's spirits lifted.

"I'll go up the west boundary and over the ridge," Liza said aloud as she crossed the yard toward the creek path. It made her feel better to talk to herself. If she said plain and sensible things, only plain and sensible things could happen to her in the night.

Outside the yard gate she stopped to look and listen. It was easy to patrol this part of the land. She walked the creek path every day and knew every turn and bump along the way. She felt very brave as she stood on this familiar bit of ground, holding

Adam's rifle in her hands. There was nothing so wonderful about watching the land.

Liza bent forward and peered up the creek. She saw the long bridge beneath the bluff and remembered the outsider called Travis Barton. Even if he was a Lumber Company man he was kind and cheerful. She wished she might meet him again right now. He would be company in the loneliness of the night.

Then, beyond the bridge, she saw the Devil's Seesaw, black and tall in the moonlight. A bright ribbon of water, lighted by the moon, moved around the base of the rock and came toward her in the creek bed. Staring at the rock and water Liza had a sudden sense that the great rock was coming toward her. It began to look different too, like a giant with his head sunk into his shoulders. Her scalp prickled and she shut her eyes.

"It's nothing at all," she said out loud.

But when she opened her eyes Liza didn't look toward the Devil's Seesaw again. She turned in the opposite direction and went up the mountain.

There was a rough path along the Mather boundary line, but it was not much used. Her father and Adam had not cleared this path as they had the others on the mountain. It was overgrown with fern and pine shoots, large enough to stumble over or brush into her eyes.

It was dark among the trees too, with only a

patchy light to see by as the wind-flung branches moved across the moonlight. Liza held the rifle in one hand and used the other to push her way past the undergrowth. She tried to walk carefully and to listen for strange sounds. But it was hard to walk and listen in the darkness. It was even harder not to think about the things she could not see among the shadows. Once she stepped on a stick and the sharp, cracking sound made her stop dead still, her heart thumping.

There was nothing to hear but the wind and the distant chuckling of the creek far below. She let out her breath in a long thankful sigh.

"Pooh," she said. She didn't say it very loud, but she felt better.

She reached the clearing at last. The moon shone full and bright in the open space and Liza sat down on a rock to rest.

"No use getting wore out," she told herself. She rested the butt end of the rifle on the ground between her feet and held tight to the muzzle with both hands. All around her were the dark and crowding trees, but it was light and safe in the clearing. Liza sat very straight and felt her courage come back to her.

"Might better bide here a time," she said. "I can see better from high up like this." She opened her eyes very wide and looked hard into the black trees. There was nothing to see. She pushed the scarf back from her ears and listened for a long time. There was only the wind to hear, but it was louder than before. The trees groaned and creaked in its rushing path.

"Might come on to storm," said Liza and a small part of her courage seemed to ooze out through her hands and feet. She looked up at the piling clouds. They were bunched and massed above her like mountains in the sky. The moon still shone in its blue space, but a heavy cloud was rolling toward it.

"Thunder clouds," said Liza in a small voice. She stood up and looked uncertainly at the moon. There would be no seeing anything once the moon was covered by that hurrying cloud.

A thudding crash came from the darkness and Liza's knees buckled beneath her. She crouched down by the rock and shut her eyes. The next second something swept past her with a bounding leap and Liza opened her eyes just in time to see a deer disappear into the trees beyond the clearing.

"O-h-h-h!" The thin wail that came from Liza's throat had no sound of courage. Her hands shook on the rifle and her knees were like jelly.

She got slowly to her feet and fought against an impulse to start running. If she took the home path she would be safe in the cabin in ten quick minutes. It was a clear path and the moon still shone to light the way. Then she shut her eyes and made herself think about Adam. He wouldn't run because he was afraid. He was a boy and had to be brave. She was a girl and she had to show that she was brave too.

"I'm staying." Her voice quivered slightly, but she shouldered the rifle and began walking very fast back and forth across the clearing. It was better than sitting still and imagining things. She began to whistle. It helped hide the wail of the wind.

"I can see and hear better in the open," she told herself. "If they come to do us harm, I can know it just as well here."

She looked up. The clouds were bigger and blacker. They were nearer the moon too.

"Maybe," said Liza shakily, "I ought to get back and see how Adam does." She stood still and thought about Adam again. She wondered what he would do if he were alone on the mountain top with a storm rising and the moon about to be hidden by the clouds.

Before she could decide what Adam might do, an owl began to hoot from the darkness of the trees behind her. Liza's hair stirred uncomfortably on her scalp.

"It's a warning," she thought. Annie Lou always said that an owl hooting in the night was a sign of sorrow. Annie Lou had been right about the weather. She might be right about the owl too. Liza took two steps toward the path that led down the mountain.

Then with a suddenness that made Liza cry aloud the clouds swept over the moon. A mutter of thunder rolled across the black sky and a thin rain pattered on the dry leaves of the clearing. Liza waited no longer. She ran.

It was no help to know the path by daylight. In the night there were queer rocks along the way and trees that held out their branches to stop her plunging flight down the mountain. Liza stumbled on, falling over the rocks and fighting her way past the clawing branches. Once she was sure she had missed the path and was lost on the mountain. Then a jagged flash of lightning lit the sky and showed her the path again. The thunder and rain came hard after the lightning, a crashing, pelting fury of sound.

At last a small square of light from the kitchen window showed through the trees and Liza gave a shout. She raced down the garden slope in a final burst of speed and flung herself against the back door.

It swung open with her weight and Liza fell across the doorsill. As she lay there, fighting for breath, a new crash of sound rolled over her. It was like thunder, but heavier than thunder, a shuddering, earth-splitting roar that seemed to crack the air. Liza moaned and put her hands over her ears.

"Adam," she whispered, "oh, Adam, wake up!"

Chapter 10

LIZA heard the door open and knew that Adam was coming back. She struggled to sit up straight, but the quilt that Adam had wrapped around her was close about her shoulders and she could not move. For a moment she wondered why she was sitting by the fire in Annie Lou's old rocker. It was pitch-black night. She ought to be in bed. Then, as Adam came forward to warm his hands at the coals, she remembered.

It was Adam's face reflected in the glow of the fire that brought everything back to her. She had seen that same look in his eyes when he found her lying on the doorstep. He had not spoken to her then or asked any questions as he led her to the fireplace.

A moment later he had left her there and gone out into the night. Liza knew that he wanted to find out if that thundering crack of sound was the trouble they were waiting for. A blasting stick would split the air that way. But real thunder, shaking the hills, sometimes made the same sound.

Now Adam was back and Liza could not wait to know what he had seen on the outside. "Was it the . . . the trouble?"

"There was nothing," said Adam. "I went over the home land and everything is as it ought to be." He sat back on his heels and frowned into the coals.

"Could be it was thunder," said Liza uneasily.

"Maybe." Adam poked at the fire, keeping his face turned from her.

Liza sat back and sighed deeply. It was warm and comfortable in the chair. With Adam nearby and the fire burning brightly she could almost believe that the fearful time on the mountain had been a dream.

"Sure is lucky Father sleeps so sound," she said after a moment.

"The thunder roused him at first," said Adam. "I was sitting up in the bed when he came out to see if all was right."

Liza's eyes widened. "Did he think to wonder where I was?" She glanced over her shoulder, half-expecting to see her father listening from the shadows.

"Don't fret," said Adam. "I told him I was rested fine and no one had to watch over me. I didn't say where you'd gone. He expected you were in your bed, I reckon."

Liza nodded. She was thinking that at least one thing Adam had said was true. He did seem better from his food and rest. His eyes were alive once more and he moved without the weary effort that had worried her during the day.

"Maybe we should go to bed," she said. Her eyelids were heavy and it was hard to keep awake.

Adam got up and took his rifle from the chimneypiece. "I'm going out. The storm's over. You go to bed."

"No!" Liza was wide awake in a moment. She kicked aside the quilt and jumped to her feet. "You hadn't ought to go out now. It's 'most morning."

"Morning!" Adam pointed to the clock. "It's barely midnight. There's more than half the night to go."

Liza stared at the clock. It wasn't possible that she had been alone on the mountain so short a time. "If you go out, I'm coming too," she said. But she was careful to say it softly. If she followed Adam he might not send her back. He might even be glad of her company though he would never ask for it.

Liza waited until Adam was off the porch before she came after him. The rain had stopped, but the wind still blew as strongly as ever and the clouds were over the moon. It was too dark to see Adam but she heard the click of the yard gate and ran toward it.

"Adam!" The wind caught the word and threw it helter-skelter into the air.

But Adam heard her. "Go back!" he shouted out of the darkness.

Liza didn't bother to answer. She ran forward and stood by Adam's side. She could see him now, a dark shape against the blackness of the trees. "I'm coming," she said and took his hand to show that she meant it.

Adam didn't move or speak.

"Seems awful quiet," she said at last. It was true. The wind roared through the trees, but there was a queer undercurrent of stillness behind its noise.

"Huh?" Adam sounded surprised.

"Quiet," said Liza. "Different somehow." She put her head on one side and listened again. "Don't you hear it? The quiet, I mean."

"You're talking crazy," said Adam impatiently. "Come on if you're set on coming and stay close."

Liza didn't need to be told to stay close. She was right at Adam's heels as they climbed the mountain. She didn't mind the darkness now or the roughness of the path. Even the wind seemed more friendly and the sudden night noises were nothing but falling branches or running animals.

They saw and heard nothing unusual on the way up the mountain. When they reached the clearing they rested for a time on the same rock where Liza had sat before that night.

"Still hearing the quiet?" asked Adam. It was the first thing he had said in nearly an hour and Liza was startled by his abrupt tone. She pretended not to hear his question and yawned instead.

"You're plumb wore out," said Adam. He spoke more gently and Liza felt better. She was tired, but she wasn't going to let Adam know it.

"I am not," she said loudly and yawned again.

"Come along." Adam took her hand and led her toward the home-bound path. Liza didn't try to hold back, even though she knew Adam was taking her home to bed. She stumbled along beside him, trying to make her feet go where she wanted them to. They felt like lumps of lead and her eyelids were nearly as heavy. They kept drooping over her eyes. It didn't matter. It was too dark to see anyhow. By the time they reached the yard Liza was walking in a half-sleep and it was only Adam's hand in hers that kept her upright.

"You . . . you . . ." Liza wanted to tell him that he shouldn't go out on the mountain again. But she couldn't make the words come. She felt Adam lift her on her bed and the wonderful warmth of the quilt as he covered her.

"You did a good job, Liza."

It was Adam's voice but it came from a long way

off. Those warming words were the last thing Liza knew before she drifted into sleep.

She was roused by a voice that spoke right in her ear. It was Seth, seated heavily on her chest with his feet on her pillow. He poked at her eyes to make her open them. Then he pulled one of her braids.

"Go 'way!" Liza tried to roll over to escape the probing fingers. But Seth was firmly seated and a solid weight. She couldn't move so she opened her eyes.

Seth's face was close to hers and his fingers were poised for another poke.

"I'm awake," she said quickly. She rolled Seth to one side so she could sit up.

For a moment she wondered why she was fully dressed. Then, as Seth struggled to right himself among the folds of her quilt, she remembered her stumbling trip down the mountain.

"Where's Adam! What time is it?" Liza got up suddenly and shook her head to clear the last sleepiness away. It must be full morning, for the gray light of a cloudy day came through her window. There were voices in the kitchen and the hum of Annie Lou's singing.

Liza gave her face and hands a hasty splash and smoothed her hair with her fingers.

"Why didn't somebody wake me up?" she demanded as she hustled Seth into his clothes. She had a sudden feeling that she had missed something

136

by oversleeping. Adam might have seen or heard more about the trouble during the night and she had wasted time sleeping. She hurried Seth through his washing so fast that his face was scarlet with the scrubbing she gave it.

"Teth hurted," he said unhappily.

Liza took time to give him a hasty kiss. "There," she said.

"Dere," said Seth and smiled at her.

It was just as Liza had feared. The whole family was up and finished with breakfast when she and Seth came into the kitchen. Her father stood at the window with Adam beside him. They had been talking, but were silent now as they looked out into the yard.

The remains of breakfast were still on the table, for Annie Lou was too busy for dishwashing. She was gathering together all the family laundry and heaping it in a big washtub in the center of the room. It was Annie Lou's way to have a sudden fit of energy on a day like this. She was bound to do the washing when there was no sun to dry the clothes.

Liza turned her back on Annie Lou's bustle and looked at Adam. If she saw his face she would know if anything had happened in the night. But her father spoke before Adam noticed her.

"Too wet for the plow," he said. "The ground is

plumb sodden and more rain likely to come. There's rain clouds right over the mountain."

"Like I said," said Annie Lou triumphantly. "Too much sun for the season."

"There's no sun now," said Liza loudly. "No sun for plowing or drying clothes either." She wanted Adam to look at her and she also wanted Annie Lou to know what she thought of washing on such a day.

Adam turned toward her and a quick unspoken message passed between them. She lifted her eyebrows in a question and he shook his head.

The relief of knowing that nothing unusual had happened in the night made Liza feel almost cheerful. But the sight of the unwashed clothes in the tub sent her spirits down again. Annie Lou had paid no attention to her remark about the weather. She had found Seth's laundry in the wardrobe and added it to the overflowing heap.

"Best to eat breakfast first," said Adam, who knew what Liza thought of helping with the family wash. "I'll help tote water from the creek."

"Can't dry clothes with no sun," said Liza as she helped Seth into his chair.

"You can string lines in the room," said her father. "There's a power of washing to do."

"Washa!" shouted Seth. "Teth help."

"You keep out of the way," muttered Liza. She knew Seth's way of helping.

138

He would be in the tub up to his ears and splashing soapy water everywhere.

"Won't," said Seth. He finished his breakfast by stuffing a whole biscuit into his mouth and pushing his bowl away. Then he lifted his arms to Liza as a sign that he wanted to get down and begin the day's work.

"Come along then," said Liza. She got the water pail and went slowly toward the door. Seth trotted after her with a teacup and Adam lifted the kettle from the crane. But even with a pail, a kettle, and Seth's cup there would be many trips from the house to the creek before the big tub was full.

Once outside, with the door shut on the hated laundry, Liza began to recover her spirits. Even though it was cold and cloudy, the air was brisk and the wind blew her ill-temper away.

"You didn't really see anything last night?" she asked as she followed Adam across the yard.

"Not a sight or sound," said Adam. "I reckon we let ourselves get too fanciful. Likely it was thunder after all."

Liza was only too willing to believe that Adam was right. In the light of day it was hard to remember how frightened she had been the night before. She skipped along after Adam, her feet slipping in the muddy yard and the pail bumping against her bare legs.

"Look at Seth!" she cried when they reached the yard gate.

Seth had stopped beside a particularly damp patch of mud and was happily scooping handfuls of wet ooze into his cup. Already his hands and face and overalls were smeared with the same mixture.

"Something else to wash," said Adam teasingly.

"You'd talk different if you had to scrub all day," said Liza and turned up her nose at him. She pushed past him and ran down the path toward the creek. Halfway down the slope she stopped and stared. Where was the creek? The stones were there, all the rocks she knew so well. But they lay in the creek bed, high and dry above the thin trickle of water that ran along the pebbly bottom.

"Adam!"

She didn't need to call him. He was beside her, staring at the creek bed just as she was.

"Wh—— what . . . ?" Liza stopped. The creek water had disappeared overnight. It was too much to wonder about all at once.

"Look!" said Adam. He choked as he spoke.

Liza looked where Adam pointed. She closed her eyes, then opened them very wide. She wanted to make sure that she really saw the Devil's Seesaw lying sideways across the mouth of the creek. It was there all right, a black mass of rock that blocked the water from Mather Creek like a dam.

"That's the quiet," she whispered, remembering

the strange stillness she had noticed the night before. It was the sound of the creek water that she had missed. Its hurrying murmur had been shut off by the Devil's Seesaw.

Adam ran toward the rock and Liza raced to catch up with him. When they reached the spot where the Devil's Seesaw had once stood they stared silently at the shattered rock that had once been a solid base for the great stone. There were patches of blackened rubble to prove that the Devil's Seesaw had been blasted from its place in order to fall across the mouth of Mather Creek. All the water had been turned aside and now poured down into the dark depths of T'Other Place.

"Who would . . . ? Why did . . . ?" Liza's questions stuttered to a stop.

"They've cut us off," said Adam. "It's the devil's work."

Liza jumped when Adam spoke. She had seen him when he was upset and worried. She knew how pale and tense he was when he was unhappy. But she had never seen him angry before. Her father was often angry. When he was, his eyes were like blue ice and his voice was hard and cold. Adam's eyes were like that now and so were his words.

"Come!" Adam almost pushed Liza off the rock in his hurry. "We must get back and tell Father."

"Tell Father!" Liza stared at Adam with her mouth open. "You can't! Think what he'll do."

But Adam paid no heed. He was already running along the creek path toward home. Liza came after him, her heart pounding at the thought of what Adam might do in his anger.

"Wait, Adam, wait!" Her voice rose in a cry of fear.

Adam stopped then to wait for her. When Liza reached his side she could not look at his eyes. The fury in them was more frightening than any of her father's angers. He spoke with an effort, trying to fight back the strength of his feeling.

"We can't keep this from Father," he said shakily. "He'd soon know the water's been cut off. I've got to tell him myself so he won't . . ."

A voice, hailing them from the direction of the Devil's Seesaw, forced Adam to a stop. He and Liza turned with one motion and saw the outsider, the man of whom Liza had thought so often in the past few days, standing by the fallen rock. "It's Mr. Barton," she said and lifted her hand in greeting.

Something struck at her arm and the next instant Adam had thrust himself forward to stand between her and the distant figure on the rock.

"Get out!"

There was no mistaking Adam's feeling. He meant what he said with all the force of his being.

"Adam!" Liza put out her hand to stop him, but Adam was past hearing. He leaned down and

picked up a stone. Holding it in his hand, poised to throw, he repeated his harsh warning.

Mr. Barton did not wait for a second invitation to leave. He jumped down behind the rock without trying to speak again.

"Adam, you hadn't ought to . . ." Liza's voice quavered to a stop. There was no use talking to Adam now. She let him take her by the arm and pull her along the path toward home.

It began to rain again before they reached the

yard gate. Liza saw her pail and the kettle lying in the path where they had been dropped, but Adam went past them as though they did not exist. There was no thought in his mind of washing or water-carrying. He wanted only to get to his father and tell him in his own way what the neighbors had done.

Seth was still playing in the mud patch when they crossed the yard and Liza was glad of an excuse to linger behind. By the time she had persuaded Seth to leave his mud pies and come in out of the rain Adam had been five minutes in the house.

She listened carefully as she scraped mud off Seth's hands and clothes, waiting for the explosion of rage that Adam's news was sure to bring. But there was no sound from inside.

"Wanna mud!" shouted Seth as Liza dragged him up the porch steps. He kicked at Liza's shins to emphasize his wish.

"Hush!" Liza put her hand over his mouth and opened the door slowly.

Her imagination had pictured her father's reaction to Adam's news in a dozen violent ways. But when Liza looked into the kitchen all her wild imaginings fell to nothing.

Her father sat at the table with his face buried in his hands. He was perfectly still, like a figure turned to stone. Adam stood beside him, looking down at his father's bent shoulders. There was no anger in Adam's face now. He seemed bewildered and almost frightened.

"He's kilt!" cried Liza.

"No," said Adam slowly. "Not kilt, only sorrowed. It's not in him to think they could act so." He moved away from the table and came close to her. "It's hit him real bad," he said. "Act natural when he rouses, as if nothing was wrong."

"What will he do?" asked Liza fearfully.

"Nothing," said Adam. "It's no time for anger. I see that now. We have to think of Father."

"There'll be water in the creek with the rain come on," said Liza hopefully. "Maybe he'll not feel so if there's water."

"All the rain there is won't wash this sorrow from him," said Adam. "It's the meanness of it, that and the unneighborly way of it."

Adam was right. In the next three days it rained without pause. The water in the creek rose to its usual level, but Dan Mather kept to himself in his room. Never once in all those long and dreary days did he speak of the neighbors' act.

The rest of the family moved quietly about the business of living. Liza helped Annie Lou with the washing without a word of complaint. Adam toted water and read in the long intervals of silence. Even Seth sensed the need for quiet. He played by himself or followed at Liza's heels as she went about her work.

Annie Lou was the only one who took a strange satisfaction in the long days of rain. Her prophecies about the weather had come true and she lost no opportunity to say so. When she was not working with Liza she rocked in her chair, moaning happily about the state of the weather. She was too occupied with her triumph to notice the uneasiness of the rest of the household.

"There'd be high tide in the creek if it wasn't for the Devil's Seesaw being fallen like it is," said Liza on the afternoon of the third day. "Maybe the rest of the hollow is flooded out."

Adam looked up from his book and shrugged. "Serve 'em right," he said indifferently. "It's not our affair."

Liza sighed. It was just after dinner. Her father had not joined them for the meal. The food waited for him on the table, growing cold in the chill of the room. Seth was sleeping on Adam's bed and Annie Lou was dozing by the dying fire. Adam was too deep in his book for company. There was nothing to do and no one to talk to. Liza sighed again.

She wished Adam would come out with her and walk up the creek to see what was happening beyond the Devil's Seesaw. It was still raining and she didn't want to go alone. Liza wandered off to the window and looked out over the sodden yard. It was a sea of mud.

There was nothing in the scene to cheer her and she was about to turn away when she saw something move in the shadow of the trees at the edge of the yard. She leaned forward to see better.

"Emmy!"

Liza was careful to say the word softly. She saw Emmy looking fearfully toward the house and moved her hand across the window pane to attract her attention.

For a moment she was not sure that Emmy saw her, then Emmy lifted her hand in a strangely appealing gesture. It was as though she wanted Liza's help and dared not ask for it.

Liza ran to the door.

Chapter 11

"Dɪᴅ your ma send you?"

Liza took Emmy by the shoulders and shook her. In the few moments since she had run from the house Emmy had not said one word to explain why she was there. She stood huddled in her shawl, with such a mixture of fright and pleading in her eyes that Liza's imagination leaped to a dozen dangers.

In an instant she pictured Mrs. Tillotson stone dead and all the little Tillotsons starving to death. Maybe something had happened to Mr. Tillotson. He might be dead too.

"What's wrong? Who's dead?" Liza shook Emmy again.

"No—— nobody," said Emmy, her teeth chattering. "Hit's Pa, him and the tide." Her lips quivered. "Ma didn't send me. I came to . . ." She couldn't finish and gestured helplessly with one hand.

"Tide! Is it flood tide?" Liza pulled her jacket closer as a gust of wind blew a heavier shower of rain about them. In spite of the cold and wet, Liza felt a warming glow of excitement. A flood tide meant disaster in the hollow. After three days of enforced quiet Liza was ready for something to happen.

"The water's near up to the porch," said Emmy tearfully. "Pa, he got hurted bad trying to set up the corner post. He got hisself in the house, but now he can't move from his chair with the hurting. Ma dassn't ask help of you because . . ." Once again Emmy stopped and stared at the ground.

Liza understood. Mrs. Tillotson was ashamed to ask for help from the Mathers. When Mr. Tillotson had cut off the water, he had also cut off all right to help and consideration from the Mathers.

"What about the Bedfords and the Lashers?" asked Liza. "If your ma dassn't ask us, why won't she ask them?"

"The tide," said Emmy shakily. "Hit's bad with them too, seeing as they live above the fork. All the hollow above the Devil's Seesaw is flooded. I didn't know if I . . . I mean, you and me used to be friends before and I . . ." Emmy was really crying now.

Liza gave Emmy a quick impulsive hug. "You did right to come," she said. "Come on. I'll go back with you."

"Get Adam," said Emmy. "He could help move Pa afore the house falls."

Liza shook her head. "He's angered," she said. "Like as not he wouldn't come and I dassn't ask Father."

Emmy pulled her shawl tighter. "Hit's awful what they done. Pa's sorry now, real sorry, and Ma, she's taking on at him something awful. She says the tide is a judgment on him and on the Bedfords and the Lashers, too, because they helped Pa with the blasting."

"Father's not angered," said Liza. "Only sorrowed. Let's not think on that now. We're wasting time. Come on."

Emmy did not try to argue. She had no chance, for Liza was running ahead of her along the mountain path.

Liza did not look back to see whether Emmy was following. The first thought in her mind was to see the tide, the great rolling sea of water that she had seen only once before in her life. Two years back the spring rains had raised the creek water to the porch steps. Now the water was no higher than usual in Mather Creek. The Devil's Seesaw had saved them from flooding by turning the water into T'Other Place.

It was hard to make sense of the strange turn of events. The neighbors had meant to harm them by cutting off their water. But their unfriendly act had become a blessing. It was too much for Liza to figure out and she gave up trying.

"Wait! Wait for me!" Emmy's voice came in a thin wail from behind.

But Liza was not far from the Tillotson land and pretended not to hear. A few steps more and she was at the edge of the trees. Then she stopped and stared.

The Tillotson cabin was near the bottom of the cleared hillside. The creek, which usually ran peacefully between high banks well below the house and yard, had become a swollen river that lapped at the doorstep of the cabin. All this wide stretch of water was filled with logs and uprooted trees that jostled and tumbled on the fast-moving tide.

Emmy clutched at her arm. "Hit's higher," she said in a sobbing whisper. "The water's over the porch. They'll be kilt! Pa!" She pulled at Liza, urging her on. "Do something!" she cried. "Liza, do something!"

Liza didn't wait to think what she might do. The hillside was a wasteland of mud and rain, but she raced down the slope, slipping and sliding over the rough wet ground. The back door was open and, even before she crossed the threshold, Liza heard Mrs. Tillotson's voice. It rose above the wind and rain and even above the running sound of the tide.

"Hit's no more than you deserve, Sam Tillotson!" shouted Mrs. Tillotson. "I told you time and again you was maddened to do such a thing. Now there's a judgment come."

Liza and Emmy were in the kitchen now, standing beside Mrs. Tillotson, who had taken a battle stand in the center of the room. The young Tillotsons clustered around her, clutching at her skirts and wailing in tune with their mother's voice. The Least 'Un was in his basket on the table. His murmuring complaints were drowned in the noise about him.

Mrs. Tillotson did not see Liza right away. There was too much sound and confusion in the room to notice one more person. She was still telling Mr. Tillotson what she thought of him. She went through the whole history of his foolishness and that of the neighbors in wanting to sell their trees for cash money. But this was nothing to their wickedness in blasting the Devil's Seesaw to cut off the Mather water. Mrs. Tillotson's face grew red and her arms flailed the air as she told of the judgment that had come upon them for this act.

The little Tillotsons shivered and paled at the force of their mother's rage. They drew closer to her skirts and peered from the protecting folds at their father.

Sam Tillotson was a pitiable sight. He sat in the big armchair with his injured leg on a footstool. His face had lost its look of ruddy health. His cheeks hung in folds, his mouth drooped open. He didn't move except to wave his hand helplessly from time to time as though Mrs. Tillotson's words were mosquitoes he wanted to brush away.

"Ma!" Emmy tugged at her mother's sleeve.

Mrs. Tillotson shook her off. "We'll all be drowned together, Sam Tillotson. The water's rose to the door and will be over the sill next. I can't heave you out of that chair and you know it. What's to be done?"

"Leave me be," whispered Sam huskily. "Leave me drown. Get out while there's time." He covered his face with his hands.

The small Tillotsons wept louder than before. Mrs. Tillotson swept them together in her arms. "Don't take on," she said softly. "We ain't leaving your pa. I'm just putting the fear of God into him for his own good. Emmy! Where's Emmy?"

Mrs. Tillotson was suddenly her usual brisk self. She had finished punishing her husband and was prepared to save him.

"Emmy!" she repeated in a shout.

"I'm here, Ma." Emmy came forward, pulling Liza after her. "Liza's come."

"Liza!" Mrs. Tillotson gave Liza a startled glance. For a second she looked confused and uncertain. Then her good sense overcame her doubts and she smiled. "Hit's a kindness to come," she said simply. "Between us maybe we can heave him out the back. He can't walk."

Liza only nodded. A small river of water was running over the front doorsill. There was no time for talk. She and Emmy grabbed Sam Tillotson by one arm and Mrs. Tillotson took the other. The young Tillotsons pulled at his good leg. It was no use. It was like trying to move a mountain.

"Git!" cried Sam suddenly. "Git while you . . . Hit's going down!" His last words were a shout as a blow struck the side of the cabin. It tilted the floor upward and the chair slid a few inches toward the back door.

Liza was thrown to the wall by the force of the blow. All the small Tillotsons were on the floor. Only Mrs. Tillotson was still on her feet, clinging to the chair.

"Hit's going for sure," she said solemnly. "Sam, I can't leave you be, no matter what you done." She bent over the back of the chair and burst into tears. The children joined her, their voices rising in a chorus of misery.

Liza stared at the frightened group, her thoughts whirling. An idea had come to her when the blow struck. For a moment in the confusion of wails and sobs she couldn't remember it. Then as Mrs. Tillotson lifted her head and gripped hard at the chair as though bracing herself for the near disaster, Liza knew what it was.

"The chair!" she shrieked and flung herself at it. "It moved! Push it out the back!"

Mrs. Tillotson didn't waste a moment. She knew instantly what Liza meant. "Push!" she cried. "Emmy, fetch the Least 'Un! Push, I say!" She leaned her great weight on the chair and heaved.

Liza helped and so did all the little Tillotsons. Emmy was already out the back door with the Least 'Un in her arms. The chair moved. Sam groaned as the footstool fell over and his bad leg hit the floor. No one paid attention. The chair was in the middle of the floor now. The back door was only a few feet away.

Then another blow hit the cabin. There was a splintering of wood and a crash as a great log wedged against the front door.

No one had breath or time for words or fear. With one impulse they grabbed at the chair, pulling, hauling, and clawing it toward the door. Sam Tillotson's eyes were closed now. His lips moved. He might be helping by prayer, but his limp weight seemed greater than ever.

"Push!" gasped Mrs. Tillotson as the chair jammed in the doorway.

"It's stuck!" Liza leaned against the door and fought for breath. There was Sam still in the chair and the chair would not go through the door. All their work was for nothing.

But Mrs. Tillotson was not beaten. "Git back!"

she shouted and pushed the children aside. Then she bent down and with a last mighty heave lifted up the chair. Sam Tillotson slid out through the door, into the rain and mud of the yard. The children and Liza came after him. Mrs. Tillotson shoved the chair aside and was safe in the yard as another log hit the outer wall. The cabin tilted forward as the porch gave way with a crash of breaking wood.

But there was no time to worry about the cabin. Liza and Mrs. Tillotson between them caught Sam Tillotson by the shoulders and dragged him through the slippery mud to the shelter of the nearest tree. They propped him against the trunk, safe above the flood.

All the family gathered close around him. The rain dripped down through the branches. Everyone was wet to the skin and shaking with the cold. Only the Least 'Un, warm and dry in his covering of blankets, was comfortable. He lay in his mother's arms and looked up into her face with round, confident eyes.

Liza and Emmy huddled together near the family group. No one spoke. The children did not even cry. They had been through too much for tears. They watched their mother. They did not look at their father. He was too miserable a sight to bring hope or comfort.

Mrs. Tillotson was the first to speak. "I thank God," she said and held the Least 'Un closer.

"Ma?" It was one of the smallest of the Tillotsons who spoke. "Ma, what's to become of us?"

Mrs. Tillotson shook her head. Sam Tillotson groaned. Emmy gave a shuddering sigh. Liza, standing close to her, heard it. She didn't stop to think. She spoke right out.

"You can take shelter with us," she said.

Chapter 12

LIZA had run halfway home along the mountain path before her breath gave out and she stopped to rest and think. She stood in the shelter of a dripping pine, huddled close to the scaly trunk. The rain had stopped in the past few minutes, but it was still cold and damp on the mountainside. She shivered and wished her jacket was not so wet.

"They're worse off than me," she said to herself as she thought of the sad and sorry family she had left under the tree in the Tillotson yard. She had blurted out her invitation without thinking of her father and Adam. Now she had to think about them.

She dug her toe into the wet pine needles. Somehow she must make them take in the Tillotsons. Of course they wouldn't like it. Sam Tillotson had done them a harm. But the harm had turned to good when the floods came. Now Sam was sorry and his leg hurt. Mrs. Tillotson and the children were just as miserable as Sam and it wasn't their fault. They couldn't stay under the tree for long. Something had to be done in a hurry.

Liza began to run again. Perhaps when she faced her father and Adam some thought would come to her that would make them do as she wished.

But Liza slowed to a walk as she came in sight of the cabin. When she reached the shed she was tempted to stop and pay a visit to Tilda. Just as she lifted her hand to push open the shed door the rain came again.

Liza turned away and dashed for the cabin. As she hesitated by the back door she remembered in a sudden gladdening flash something that she had not taken into her thoughts until now. It was what Mrs. Tillotson had said to her after she had given her invitation.

"It is what your mother would do."

Mrs. Tillotson had spoken quietly, almost in a whisper. Liza had not had time to think what she meant then. It was a time for action, not thoughts. But the memory of her mother was warm within her as she opened the back door.

Adam was still reading at the table and her father's plate of food was just where she had left it. Annie Lou slept in her chair and Seth was still beneath the quilt on Adam's bed. For a moment Liza wondered if she had ever left the kitchen. The violent activity at the Tillotsons was almost unreal in the cheerless quiet and sameness of the room.

"Adam!"

Liza spoke sharply. She had a sudden wish to startle him. While she had been on an errand of mercy he had done nothing but stay as she had left him.

Adam looked up. "What? What's that?" He blinked as the world of his book faded. Then he frowned. "Where'd you go?"

But Liza was not ready to tell him about the Tillotsons yet.

"Father should come and eat," she said. She glanced at the cold food and at the ashes in the fireplace. "Fire's near out. It's cold in here." She spoke as though the dead fire and the untouched food were Adam's fault. She was still annoyed that he had been sitting over a book while the Tillotsons were cold and forlorn in the rain.

Adam put his book aside and rose slowly from the table. As he stirred up the fire he watched Liza with a sort of puzzled surprise.

"You're wet through," he said after a minute.

"Hm," said Liza. She had taken the plate from the table and dumped its contents back into the big pot. In the next few minutes she must make her father come out of his room so she could tell him what she had done. He would hear her news better with hot food before him.

Liza moved fast. The bustle she made roused Annie Lou. Her chair crackled and rustled as she moved among her treasures.

"Rain's got in my bones," muttered Annie Lou. "Hit'll come on to flood tide, just like I said."

"The tide's come already," said Liza. She was dusting the crumbs from the table when her father came.

"You saw it?" Adam sat back on his heels and looked hard at Liza.

Liza nodded. She had no time for words, for Seth was awake and calling her. When she went to lift him up she saw that his face was streaked with the remains of his dinner and the dust he had rolled in that morning.

"You're a sight for sure," she said and hugged him.

Liza scrubbed Seth's face and hands. Time was slipping away. What could she do to make her father and Adam understand what must be done? She thought again of her mother as she poked Seth's legs into clean overalls. Her mother would have known what to do. The Tillotsons would be safe and warm inside the cabin if her mother were here to manage things.

She looked at the table as she let Seth slide off her lap. He trotted off to help Adam with the fire as

161

she stared at the empty tin plate at her father's place. The whole table looked bare and forlorn with nothing pretty or womanlike about it.

Liza shut her eyes, trying to picture the room and table as they were when her mother was living. The minutes ticked away and the rain drummed on the roof. There was no roof over the Tillotsons. They were waiting for her to provide one.

"Adam!" Liza leaped to her feet, her eyes shining. She had remembered. She knew now what her mother had done to make it pleasant to sit at the table. She must hurry. Her father might come for his dinner at any moment. Even his sorrow could not keep him from his food much longer.

Adam stood up when she shouted his name. He was beside her when she ran to the cupboard and yanked open the door.

"The plates!" she cried. "Get 'em down, Adam!" She pointed to the top shelf. It was here that her mother had kept the china plates, the ones with the red roses and the flecks of gold. They had been on the shelf since her death. It was easier to wash the tin plates. But Liza remembered that it was the china plates that had made the table pretty.

"What's got into you?" demanded Adam. But he reached for the plates.

Liza was too busy to answer. She arranged a place for her father. She thought of the handful of bloodroot that she had picked the day before the

162

rains came. The frail blossoms were in a cup in her room. Her mother had kept flowers on the table. Liza got the bloodroot and set the cup on the table exactly in the middle.

"There," she said.

"It's like it used to be," said Adam. He smiled at Liza, but he still looked puzzled.

Annie Lou began to rock uneasily in her chair. She muttered and murmured to herself when she saw the table. "Hit's her," she said. "She's come back like I said."

Liza didn't mind Annie Lou's wandering talk now. She had no time to think of it, for Seth had come to inspect the china plate. His hands were already reaching for it.

"That's Father's," she said and snatched him away.

"What's mine?"

Liza was glad she had Seth to fuss with at this moment. Her father had come into the room so quietly that she had not known he was there until he spoke. Now as she settled Seth in his corner with his corncob baby and an assortment of clothespins she could pretend she had not heard his question.

When she turned back to the table her father was already seated at his place. She saw him touch one of the red roses on the plate. He didn't say anything but his eyes were remembering.

"Dinner's over and done with," said Annie Lou

sharply. She had forgotten the change in the room. She only wanted to make herself noticed. "My rheumatism's real bad," she added and groaned.

"Sit nearer the fire," said Liza. "Adam, pull up the chair."

Adam did as he was told. There was something in the way Liza spoke that was strange even to her. She felt suddenly that she had a right to speak so. It was she who had found the room cold and forlorn. She had stirred it to warmth and activity. Her mother had done such things and Liza knew that she could do them too.

She said nothing as she filled the china plate with hot food. It was her place to be silent now and serve her father. When she put the plate in front of

him he looked up at her. His eyes had lost some of their sadness and Liza's heart skipped a beat. The moment was near. But still she waited. Her father must eat first and she must prepare him for what she had to say.

"I was out in the rain," she said as she sat down near her father.

Adam sat opposite her. Liza did not look at him. She watched her father instead. It was he who must give the answer she wanted.

"Must be nigh on to flood tide," said Dan Mather and began to eat.

"It's all flooded out above the fork." Liza's hands tightened together in her lap. "The Devil's Seesaw saved us. The . . . the neighbors are . . ."

"Neighbors!" Dan Mather's voice was harsh, but he kept on eating.

"Some neighbors," said Adam bitterly.

Liza frowned at Adam. "They're people," she said. "They're flooded out. The Tillotsons are . . ."

"Sam Tillotson?" Dan Mather put down his fork and half rose from his chair.

Liza didn't dare look at him now. She stared at the bloodroot in the center of the table and talked very fast. And she told everything. She didn't stop when her father turned away from the table to pace the floor. She kept right on when Adam muttered that it "served Sam Tillotson right." She was nearly at the end of her story. In another minute she would have to say that she had asked the Tillotsons to take shelter in the cabin.

". . . and so there's only the tree to keep off the rain," she said at last.

She hesitated, knowing that her father had stopped his restless pacing and was looking at her. So was Adam. It was very quiet in the room. Even Annie Lou's chair was still. She was listening too. Seth sucked his thumb in his corner and stared at her with solemn eyes. He knew that something unusual was happening.

A sudden gust of wind blew a sheet of rain against the window. Liza stood up and faced her father. "I told Mrs. Tillotson to take shelter with us," she said clearly. "I told her Adam and maybe you would come to help with Mr. Tillotson. I told her that."

No one spoke or moved. Everyone stared at Liza, Adam with surprise and disbelief, Annie Lou with bewilderment, and Seth with no understanding at all. But Liza saw only her father's eyes. There was nothing sad or cold in them now. They were watchful and alive. But still he did not speak.

Suddenly Liza stamped her foot hard on the floor. "They're waiting!" she cried. "They're waiting in the cold and rain! Father! It's what my mother would do."

Dan Mather came forward to the table and looked down at the china plate with the red roses and the flecks of gold. Then he brushed his hand once across his eyes.

"Adam," he said, "get quilts and two of the long bean poles."

"Father!" Liza held her father's arm in a close, tight hold.

For a moment his hand rested on her head, then he turned away and followed Adam out the door.

Chapter 13

"It's hard to think it's all so different."

Liza knew what Emmy meant. They were sitting together on the porch steps in the comforting warmth of the morning sun. The sky was a pure and cloudless blue and a light wind stirred the air. After the wet and cold of the last few days it was hard to believe in the beauty of the day.

"Those kids!" Liza looked down into the yard. The rain had made it a sea of mud. Little rivers of water ran down the slope to the creek bank. The young Tillotsons and Seth were building dams with sticks and stones. They were covered with mud and perfectly happy.

Emmy smoothed down her skirt and sighed. "They'll have to be washed again," she said.

"Remember how they got washed last night?" asked Liza.

Emmy shuddered. "Don't think on it. I don't want to remember it ever again."

But Liza knew that she would never forget the Tillotsons' arrival at the cabin. It had been just on the edge of dark when they came. She had done what she could to make ready for them. She had heated water and brought out the big washtub.

Annie Lou had been made to understand that company was coming and that everyone was wet and cold and hungry. Once she knew she could be useful, Annie Lou had stirred up the pot and sorted over her store of quilts, all the ones she had made and saved through the years. She forgot her aching bones. When she heard that Sam Tillotson had hurt his leg she got out her little pots and jars of herb salve. Annie Lou was sure her herb salve could cure anything, even bones that might be broken.

Seth did what he could to get ready for the Tillotsons. He dressed his corncob baby in a clean rag and went to the door a dozen times to watch for them.

They came at last. Sam Tillotson was first through the door. He was carried in by Adam and Dan Mather on the bean-pole stretcher and settled in a chair in a corner of the room. He lay back in the chair and closed his eyes. He did not move or speak, not even when Annie Lou came to hover over him with herb salve and sounds of sympathy.

Dan Mather and Adam stood at the far side of

169

the room. They did not speak either. No one had a chance to talk, for Mrs. Tillotson with the Least 'Un in her arms and the shivering young Tillotsons crowding close to her side was in the kitchen. In an instant she was in charge of everything. There was nothing for anyone to do but obey her orders. Liza and Emmy rushed to do as they were told. The men stood back and watched. This was a time for woman's work.

The children were stripped to the skin and plunged into the tub. Emmy and Liza scrubbed and dried them. Mrs. Tillotson fed them from the big pot. Then each one was rolled into a quilt and set down upon the hearth. Seth insisted on being washed, fed, and rolled too. No one noticed that there was an extra child. He was added to the row of quilted bundles on the hearth. Five minutes later there was not a sound or motion from any child. They were all asleep, warm, full, and comfortable before the fire.

It was then that Mrs. Tillotson had time for Sam. She stood in the center of the room with her hands on her hips and spoke her mind.

"Sam!"

Sam Tillotson opened his eyes, saw his wife, and closed them again. Annie Lou murmured sympathetically but her words were lost as Mrs. Tillotson began to talk.

"His leg ain't broke. I felt it over real good and

wrapped it tight in a rag. Hit's pulled like. Sam, what you got to say?"

Sam moaned. Dan Mather took one step toward the door. Adam was right behind him. They knew what Mrs. Tillotson wanted Sam to say and they could not bear to hear it. Emmy and Liza crouched by the hearth. They were sorry for Mr. Tillotson too. But Mrs. Tillotson was bound to have her way.

"Stay, Dan Mather," she said.

Dan Mather stopped by the door.

"Sam," said Mrs. Tillotson again and her voice was loud and firm.

There was no help for him now. Sam Tillotson opened his eyes and looked at his wife. There was no comfort to be had from her. He turned to Dan Mather and at last he spoke.

"I ain't deserving of your kindness," he said slowly. His heavy face was red with the agony of his feeling. "After what I done to you there was no call for you to take notice of me and mine."

Dan Mather shook his head. Adam stared at the floor and scraped his foot along a crack between the boards. Liza turned her back to the room and poked at the fire. She wanted to hear but she could not bear to watch.

"Go on, Sam. Say it out." Mrs. Tillotson tapped her foot and waited.

Sam stared at the wall beside him and talked to it. But he said what lay heavy on his heart. "I was maddened," he said brokenly. "Thinking of the cash money near drove me mad. I was wrong, Dan Mather, and I know it now. Hit's like that Barton feller said when he come to talk to us. He says it don't do for neighbors to be unfriendly."

Dan Mather frowned as Sam mentioned Mr. Barton, but he did not try to interrupt. He waited with the others for Sam to finish what he had to say.

"Can you find it in your heart to forgive me, Dan Mather?" asked Sam. The words were out at

last and they seemed to strengthen Sam. He sat up straighter in his chair and became a man again.

Liza watched her father, holding her breath as she waited for his answer. He did not move or speak for a long minute. Then Adam touched his arm in a gesture that told what he wanted him to do. Liza wanted it too. She got slowly to her feet and went toward him.

"Wait!" Dan Mather spoke with an effort, but the hard lines around his mouth relaxed and softened. "I forgive you freely," he said slowly. "You are welcome to this house, you and yours together."

For a moment the room was quiet. Then Mrs. Tillotson let out her breath in a long sigh of relief.

"Well," she said. "That's real handsome, Dan Mather. I couldn't ask for more nor Sam either."

Everyone found a place to sleep at last. Emmy and Liza shared the same bed and Adam lay down by the fire to watch over the sleeping children. The Tillotsons took his bed. The house was quiet with sleep and no one knew when the rain stopped in the night. The bright sun of the morning was like the start of a new life. They were friends and neighbors once more and the dark days of rain and bad feeling were over.

Liza thought of these things as she sat on the steps with Emmy. It was fine to be out in the sun with Emmy beside her and the sounds of Mrs.

Tillotson's activity coming from the house. Mrs. Tillotson had driven everyone out the minute breakfast was over. Only Annie Lou and the Least 'Un were allowed to stay inside and watch the bustle of her housecleaning. Even Sam's chair had been set outside the back door where he could sit in the sun and rest his leg on the woodblock.

"The place needs redding up for sure," Mrs. Tillotson had announced. "You're not the housekeeper your ma was, Liza Mather. Git now, you and Emmy both. You're in my way."

Liza was only too glad to get away from cleaning house. But she wished Mrs. Tillotson hadn't compared her to her mother when her father could hear. He had looked at her for a moment and then turned away without speaking.

"Maybe we ought to help your ma," she said as the sounds of activity grew louder in the kitchen.

"Hm," said Emmy. She wasn't listening to Liza. She was twirling her soft hair about her fingers, pressing and patting it into curls.

Liza felt better. Maybe there was no real need to help. Her father wouldn't know whether she was working or not. He had gone with Adam along the mountain path to the Tillotsons. They wanted to see what damage the tide had done and whether the cabin was fit to live in again.

"Let's do something," said Liza. "Let's go along

174

the creek bank and look at the flood from the bluff."

"No!" Emmy shivered. "I don't want to see a flood ever again. Besides, it's all muddy by the creek. We'll get dirty." She patted her skirt with her soft plump hands.

Liza shrugged her shoulders impatiently. Sometimes it was hard to understand Emmy. She never wanted to do exciting things and she was always afraid of getting dirty. "Well, I'm going," she said after a moment. "You can stay here if you want."

She jumped to her feet and was off the steps in two long leaps. Seth saw her as she ran across the yard. Generally he wanted to go everywhere she did. But now he was too absorbed in his earthworks to do more than wave a mud-caked hand at her.

"You stay there and be good!" shouted Liza. "I'll be right back."

"Won't," said Seth.

But Liza was sure he did not mean it. He was up to his knees in a mudhole and safely stuck for a while.

From the yard gate Liza looked down at the creek. It had risen above its usual bed and raced in a brown and muddy torrent halfway up the bank. The creek path was buried under the flood, so Liza went along the top of the bank, fighting her way past brambles and branches.

"Wait! Wait for me!"

Emmy's plaintive wail came from behind her and Liza stopped. She had to wait some minutes for Emmy to catch up, for every bramble and briar was a threat to Emmy's progress.

"Why'd you come?" demanded Liza when Emmy at last reached her side. "I thought you hated to get dirty."

"No fun sitting alone," said Emmy. She rubbed at a mud streak on her skirt.

"Well, come on then," said Liza. It was hard to be cross with Emmy. She always changed her mind and did what Liza wanted in the end. No matter how slow she was and how much she fussed about unimportant things like spots on her dress, she was the kind of friend to have. "We can climb up on the bluff and see the flood from there."

Emmy was only too glad to leave the uncertainties of the bank and follow the rough path that led along the mountainside to the bluff. It was wet among the trees. Pine branches, heavy with rain, slapped at them and drenched them in a shower of drops. Within five minutes they were soaked through.

"I'm cold," said Emmy and sniffed.

"There'll be sun on the bluff," said Liza encouragingly. "We're almost there." She pushed aside an overhanging branch and held it for Emmy. "Look!"

The bluff was just ahead, a green and sunlit carpet beyond the trees. They ran forward and stood at the farthest edge where they could look down on the fork and the Devil's Seesaw. The flood spread all across the hollow above the fork. Branches, uprooted trees, and even a part of a rooftop floated down and came to rest in a tangled mass against the great stone.

"Hit's awful," said Emmy in a whisper. "Maybe that's our roof."

"Couldn't be," said Liza. "Your roof's got tar paper and this one's got shingles. See how that Seesaw holds everything back! Most of the water's going down T'Other Place."

Emmy leaned carefully forward to look. "I don't see how any water gets past to your creek. What makes it?"

Liza shook her head. "I don't know, but I sure . . ."

"Hit's a miracle what did it, young lady."

Emmy gave a little scream as Liza whirled in the direction of the voice behind them. Mr. Bedford stood at the inner edge of the bluff. Mr. Lasher was with him. Both men were wet about the shoulders and muddy to the knees. But they looked cheerful and nodded at them with easy friendliness.

"Kind of startled you some," said Mr. Bedford. He rested his thumbs in his belt and grinned.

Liza stared. The last time she had seen Mr. Bedford he had been in a black anger with her father. He had helped to blast the Devil's Seesaw across Mather Creek in revenge. Now he was smiling at her as though nothing had happened. Mr. Lasher wasn't smiling, but he looked easy and unashamed too.

"Wh—— what . . . ?" Liza couldn't go on.

"Don't blame you for wondering what I mean by a miracle," said Mr. Bedford. He paid no attention to Liza's stare or Emmy's open-mouthed surprise. He came forward to the edge of the bluff and jabbed a finger down toward the fork. "See that there stone?"

Liza nodded. She wondered how Mr. Bedford dared mention the Devil's Seesaw after what he had done.

"Hit's a miracle like I said. Ain't it so?" He nudged Mr. Lasher, who had come to stand beside him.

"Yup," said Mr. Lasher.

"And so I told your pa when I seen him this morning up to Tillotsons'. I told him . . ."

"You spoke to him?" asked Liza in a faint whisper. She couldn't imagine Mr. Bedford talking to her father with this friendly good nature. How had he dared speak to him at all?

"I sure did," said Mr. Bedford. "Oh, I had to talk him around a mite. But he come to my way of thinking. Hit's this way. The whole thing is a stand-off. You see that rock, don't you?"

Liza could only nod.

"You know how it saved you and yours from flooding out, don't you?" Mr. Bedford was plainly enjoying himself. He rocked back and forth on his heels, his thumbs still hooked in his belt.

Liza didn't try to answer. She just listened and wondered. Emmy was listening too, but she stayed close at Liza's side.

"Now we come to the miracle," said Mr. Bedford and nudged Mr. Lasher's ribs. "You look down there." He pointed once again at the Devil's Seesaw.

Liza looked but she didn't see anything that was anything like a miracle.

"Don't you get it?" Mr. Bedford laughed as Liza shook her head. "I'll tell you. The flood water's washed away the side of the bank by the stone. That's what's sending the water down your creek, not flood water, just enough to keep the creek full. That's the miracle. If that Seesaw warn't there to hold the tide water back you'd be flooded out for sure. Hit's a favor to you the stone's where it is and so I told your pa. He done us a favor and we done him one. Hit's a stand-off like I said." Bedford finished with a satisfied nod at the Devil's Seesaw.

"Stand-off?" Liza found her voice at last.

"Sure thing. Your pa saved us from ruin and we

saved him. We got high water all right and the Lashers too, but nothing like the ruin it might of been. Your pa saved the hollow."

"He sure did," said Mr. Lasher solemnly.

Liza frowned. She had no idea what Mr. Bedford was talking about. How had her father saved the hollow? She had no chance to find out, for Mr. Bedford was talking again.

"Your pa's a hard man, but he knows what he's about and I'm sure glad it's all right and friendly again between us. I was talking this forenoon to that outside feller and he says as how it's only right and proper for neighbors to be friendly-like and . . ."

"You talked to Mr. Barton!" Liza stared at Mr. Bedford and wondered how it was that Mr. Barton seemed on such good terms with all the neighbors in the hollow.

But Mr. Bedford did not like interruptions. He frowned at Liza and went right on talking as though she had not spoken.

"It's been agreed that there's to be a working on the Tillotson house and . . ." He paused and nodded at Emmy. "Never you fear, young lady. We're on our way now to tell your pa the good news. Your house is going to be all right once we get through with the working. Hit's kind of shook up and the porch washed clean away, but nothing that can't be fixed."

Emmy nodded. She was too overcome by Mr. Bedford's breezy good will to show any feeling about her house.

Liza wasn't thinking about the Tillotson cabin. The idea that Mr. Bedford felt free to walk into her father's house was enough to think about.

"You're going *there?*" she asked.

"Sure am," said Mr. Bedford cheerfully. "Got to tell Sam about the working. Your pa and Adam's gone to see the ruin. Well, got to get along."

"Mr. Bedford!" Liza had to shout, for both men were already at the edge of the trees. If Mr. Bedford was not wandering in his mind as she feared, this ruin he spoke of had something to do with her father's saving the hollow. She had to find out what it all meant.

"Yup?" Mr. Bedford turned to look at her.

"Where's the ruin?"

By way of an answer Mr. Bedford jerked his thumb toward the top of the mountain. "Go see for yourself," he said and disappeared among the trees.

Chapter 14

"I DON'T get it."

Emmy was the first to speak in the surprised silence that followed Mr. Bedford's suggestion that they find out for themselves what he meant by the "ruin."

"Me neither," said Liza, "but I'm going to find out." Mr. Bedford had pointed toward the mountaintop. It must be in that direction that the ruin lay. "Come on," she said, taking Emmy by the arm. "Let's go."

But Emmy held back. "Hit's all wet up there," she said unhappily. "We'll get all . . ."

"Pooh," said Liza. "What of it? I'm going. You stay here if you want to."

This was no choice for Emmy. It was far better to follow Liza than be left alone on the bluff. She was right at Liza's heels as they started up the mountain.

"There's a path beyond," said Liza as she pushed through a tangle of tough leatherwood. "It'll be easier going then."

"Sure hope so," said Emmy. She had just ripped a long tear in her skirt and a briar was caught in her hair. "Ouch!" She sniffed dolefully.

Liza stopped to help Emmy free her hair. It was always slow going when Emmy was with her.

She found the path a few minutes later, after only two more stops to help Emmy out of trouble. Once Emmy stumbled into a foxhole and was sure she had broken her leg. The second time she scratched her cheek on a blackberry vine and had to be told that she wasn't going to die of blood poisoning.

"You sure can get in fixes," said Liza as she mopped Emmy's cheek with the hem of her skirt.

"I can't help it," said Emmy.

She sounded close to tears, so Liza gave her shoulder an encouraging pat. "Never mind. The clearing's up ahead. Look, you can see the top of the ridge." She pointed to a line of rocks that showed faintly through the trees.

Liza had expected to find her father and Adam at the clearing. But when she and Emmy reached the open space there was nothing to see but the patchy grass, pine needles, and scattered rocks.

There was no living thing in sight except a squirrel that frisked across a rock and disappeared in a clump of evergreens.

"Sure nice to be in the sun," said Emmy, shaking out her skirt.

"Hm," said Liza. She was glad of the warming sun too after the dampness of the mountainside. But she was more interested in finding her father and Adam. "Where'd they go?"

"Who?" Emmy was smoothing her hair now.

"Adam and my father!" Liza shouted in her impatience. It was just like Emmy to come all this way and not know why she had come.

"Here!"

Adam's voice hailed her from the ridge. But she didn't waste time letting herself be surprised. She dashed toward the thin line of trees that separated the clearing from the ridge. Emmy came behind her more slowly, still smoothing and patting herself into neatness.

Adam was sitting alone on the crest of the ridge, staring down into the next hollow with his shoulders hunched and his hands clasped about his knees.

"Where's Father?" demanded Liza as she scrambled up the steep side of the ridge.

Adam only jerked his head to one side. But Liza understood that her father had taken the mountain path for home.

"What are you sitting there for?" Liza was nearly at the top of the ridge now. One more reach and pull and she would be at Adam's side.

"Looking and thinking," said Adam.

He spoke so strangely that Liza gave him a quick glance as she grasped the edge of the rock on which he sat.

"I can't get up!" Emmy was calling from the foot of the rock, but Liza pretended not to hear. She was at the top of the ridge at last and the next moment she forgot everything but the amazement of what lay before her.

"Wh—— where . . . ?" She didn't try to finish. There were no words or questions for the fact that the hollow beyond the ridge had disappeared. It had become a river, a wide, mud-brown river that washed against the treeless slopes in a moving flood. There were no cabins, no people, or any living thing. It was all water and waste.

"The ruin," said Liza when she at last found her voice.

Adam nodded. "It's what our hollow would be if Father had let the trees be cut. Here it's all washed down to rock and stumps with no trees to hold the land. It's a ruin for sure."

Liza gripped at the edge of the rock to steady herself. It made her dizzy to look at the rolling water. "Where's the people?" she asked. "Are they kilt in the flood?"

"Mr. Bedford says not," said Adam. "He says they got out in time but had to leave all behind them. The land is gone and they can't come back to bare rock. That's what it'll be when the water goes down."

"I'm falling! Catch me!"

Emmy's voice forced her to turn away from the horrible fascination of the flood. She reached down to catch Emmy's hand, but Adam was before her. With one strong pull he hoisted Emmy up to the rock beside him. Then it was Emmy's turn to stare. Her eyes grew round and her mouth fell open. She didn't say a word.

Liza had recovered from her first surprise and a crowd of questions needed to be answered. "Why'd Father go along home? What did he say to Mr. Bedford? He told us . . . Mr. Bedford, I mean . . . about the stand-off. What did Father say?"

Adam looked at her and smiled faintly. "Nothing can stop your talking, Liza Mather, not even ruin. You're as bad as Mr. Bedford. Look there!" He pointed to an uprooted tree stump at the fringe of the water.

Both Emmy and Liza saw a tattered, mud-soaked Wish Book caught among the roots of the stump. Liza said nothing. There was no need to say useless things now. But Emmy looked ready to cry.

"No good to take on," said Adam. He spoke kindly and patted Emmy's shoulder. "No good to sit looking at this any more either. Come along. Father couldn't stand to look. That's why he went on home."

Adam and Liza between them helped Emmy off the rock and back to the clearing. Now that they were out of sight of the ruin Liza pulled at Adam's sleeve.

"Mr. Bedford," she said.

Adam knew what she meant. His eyes lighted in a smile. "It's all right. He and Mr. Lasher were at the Tillotsons' when we got there. Mr. Bedford's a talker all right. He's real . . ." Adam frowned. "There's a word for him. If I had my dictionary book I'd know what it was."

Liza moved her shoulders uncomfortably. She didn't want to think how the dictionary money had been spent. "Then Father isn't mad at Mr. Bedford any more?" she asked quickly.

"Not much, I reckon. You can't be mad with an old fool like Mr. Bedford, not when he gets talking. Anyway there's going to be a working at the Tillotsons' and things will come out right with everybody working together to build up the cabin."

"Let's get back to the house," said Liza. "Race you down the path!"

She started off at a run, but Adam did not take up her challenge. He stayed behind to help Emmy over the rough places at her slower pace.

When Liza reached the garden she was far ahead. She ran down the muddy slope, past the shed, and into the front yard. The Tillotson children and Seth were nowhere in sight, but sounds of shrieking and splashing from inside the house told how Mrs. Tillotson was dealing with them.

"More washing," said Liza and sighed. She knew she ought to help Mrs. Tillotson, but her feet dragged as she went up the porch steps.

"Mr. Mather!"

The voice came from the yard gate and Liza recognized it at once. She turned, her hand lifted in warning, as Mr. Barton opened the gate and came forward.

"I want to see Mr. Mather," he said and smiled at Liza.

"Who wants to see me?"

Liza saw her father at the door and knew by the sound of his words that the stranger was no more welcome than he had ever been.

"Mr. Mather?" Mr. Barton was still walking forward.

"I'm having no truck with outsiders," said Dan Mather. "Get from my land."

Suddenly the porch and doorway were filled and crowded with people. Everyone inside wanted to be outside to see and hear. Mr. Bedford with Mr. Lasher at his elbow stood behind Dan Mather. Mrs. Tillotson and Annie Lou were in the door-

way. Sam Tillotson's face was at the window. Seth and the little Tillotsons pushed under elbows and through legs to stand where they would miss nothing. No one spoke. They were waiting for Mr. Barton to have the next word.

But Mr. Barton was too surprised to speak right away. He stood near the bottom of the porch steps and stared up at the many pairs of eyes that were watching him. He lost his chance for the next word in that short silence. Mrs. Tillotson began to talk and she knew how to make her voice heard.

"Hit's not what you think, Dan Mather. You listen to me."

The group on the porch stirred and shifted when Mrs. Tillotson spoke. It had to, for she was pushing her way forward to the edge of the porch. She stepped on one of the smaller Tillotsons, but paid no heed to his shrill cry of pain.

"You listen like I say, Dan Mather." Mrs. Tillotson had reached his side and now she took his arm in a firm grip. "What ails you treating a stranger so?" She shook his arm not at all gently.

"I'll not have outsiders from the Lumber Company coming again to break the peace." Dan Mather did not look at Mrs. Tillotson. He glared at Mr. Barton.

"Lumber Company!" Mrs. Tillotson put her hands on her hips and prepared to speak her mind. "Mr. Barton is no Lumber man. He's come to . . ."

"Perhaps I can explain," said Mr. Barton as Mrs. Tillotson paused to draw breath. "I've been hoping for a chance to talk with Mr. Mather but . . ."

"Best to let me tell him," said Mrs. Tillotson, who was now in full voice once more. She motioned Mr. Barton to silence and turned to Dan Mather.

Liza had a quick moment of disappointment when Mrs. Tillotson started talking again. Mr. Barton had a nice voice. It was quiet and confident, just as she remembered it. Mrs. Tillotson's voice was not quiet, but she knew what she wanted to say.

"Mr. Barton here has been around these parts for more than a week waiting for a chance to talk with you, Dan Mather. He's spoke to the rest of us here in the hollow and he's got something to say that's agreeable to us. If you wasn't so prideful you'd . . ."

"He's not prideful," muttered Liza indignantly.

"What's that?" Mrs. Tillotson frowned at Liza.

"He's not prideful like you say," said Liza. If she had to listen to Mrs. Tillotson she at least wanted to hear things that were true.

"Perhaps if I . . ." Mr. Barton tried to speak, but he was interrupted once again. Adam, with Emmy trailing after him, appeared around the corner of the house. It took a moment for Adam to grasp what was happening, then with one bound he was up the steps and standing beside his father. "What's wanted?" he asked, looking straight at Mr. Barton.

"Just a chance for me to set things straight," said Mrs. Tillotson forcefully. "I'm trying to tell your pa that Mr. Barton here has been waiting to . . . Emmy, you stay quiet!"

Emmy, who had only now realized that something unpleasant might happen, had given a little cry of alarm. When her mother spoke she put her hand over her mouth and stared fearfully at Mr. Barton.

Suddenly Liza wanted to laugh. Now that she knew Mr. Barton was not from the Lumber Company there was nothing to fear from her father's anger. Everybody looked so queer crowded together on the porch, with the little Tillotsons and Seth peering from behind their knees and elbows. Even Mr. Barton was almost funny, standing as he was with mud on his shoes and his hat in his hand. A bubble of laughter burst from her throat and in an instant a dozen pairs of eyes were staring at her.

"Liza!" Her father's voice was dark with disapproval.

"Laughing like a loon!" said Mrs. Tillotson.

"Yes'm," said Liza and choked back another laugh.

While Mrs. Tillotson was glaring at Liza Mr. Barton started to talk. He knew enough now to talk fast and not to stop for breath.

"I'm glad to talk with you at last, Mr. Mather," he said firmly. "I've been in the area some time making a survey at Mrs. Mather's request. She wrote the State Department of Education over a year ago to . . ."

Even Mr. Barton's voice could not rise above Annie Lou's shrill cry. She had begun to wail in a long and continuing note of fear. "Hit's come! Hit's the message come from her!" She repeated the words again and again as she rocked back and forth in the doorway.

Mr. Barton took a deep breath and almost shouted to make himself heard. "Mrs. Mather wrote to ask if a school could not be established in the area to . . ."

"School!" cried Adam. Then he stared at Mr. Barton with such a wondering hope that Liza's heart twisted within her.

She had listened to all that Mr. Barton said about where he came from and the letter he had received from her mother almost as though it was a story in a book. But when Adam cried out that single word the story was suddenly real.

"A school? A school in the hollow?" She looked hard at Mr. Barton to make sure that he meant what he said.

He nodded and was about to speak again when Dan Mather cleared his throat with a harsh sound. "A letter from my wife?" He sounded as though he didn't believe in the letter.

"Hit's the message," moaned Annie Lou. "Hit's the . . ."

"Quiet, woman!" Dan Mather seldom spoke roughly. But now he wanted an answer to his question. He stepped to the edge of the porch to hear better.

"We received it several months ago," said Mr. Barton. "I answered her letter but . . ."

"Hit's come. Hit's the message from her!" Annie Lou was shrieking now. All the people on the porch murmured and shifted uneasily at the wildness of her voice.

"Didn't you get my letter?" asked Mr. Barton when Annie Lou's words faded into a moan.

Dan Mather shook his head. He still looked suspicious. "No letter has come to us since my wife . . ." He stopped and shook his head. "I don't know about a letter," he said stiffly.

Liza saw the doubt in her father's eyes and the pain that the mention of her mother had brought. She also saw Adam's face, white and strained with a wonderful hope. She knew he was thinking of the possibility of a school. Her mother had written to Mr. Barton about starting a school in the hollow. Mr. Barton had answered her letter. Where was it?

"The message. Hit's come." Annie Lou's voice was only a murmur, but it sounded clearly in the silence that followed Dan Mather's last words.

A sudden wild thought flashed into Liza's head. It was like a great light that made everything clear and wonderfully simple. She wasted no time with words. She leaped up the steps and plunged into the crowd on the porch, pushing arms and shoulders aside and stepping over the smaller bodies of Seth and the young Tillotsons. She was headed for the door and she didn't care how rude she was about getting there.

"Liza, where you going?" Mrs. Tillotson spoke

crossly, for she was still unhappy about not telling Mr. Barton's story herself.

Liza pretended not to hear. She thought only of Annie Lou's chair, the old, deep-seated rocker with its cushions stuffed with papers, rags, bundles, and scraps.

"Let me by," said Liza when she reached the doorway. She pushed Annie Lou aside as gently as her hurry would let her. "I've got to get the message in the . . ."

She didn't finish, for Annie Lou twisted away from her and darted toward her chair. She moved fast, but Liza reached the chair first.

"Let it be!" cried Annie Lou, pulling at Liza's arm. "Leave it lay quiet."

But Liza snatched up the cushion. A shower of papers and rags fell about her feet as she clawed through the tumbled rubbish and through the cloth bag hanging on the old chair.

"Hit's safe," moaned Annie Lou. "I kept it safe from harm." She reached toward a corner of the rocker.

Once again Liza was too quick for her. She had the crumpled envelope in her hand when she turned to face her father and the others who had crowded after her into the room.

Chapter 15

"So it's true."

Dan Mather had been first to read the letter. It was addressed to his wife and it was his right to open the bent and twisted envelope and read the message inside. He was not a quick reader, and long before he had worked his way through the few lines of typewritten words Liza was dancing with impatience.

Adam stood beside her but he did not move. He watched his father, his face tense and waiting.

"Of course it's true," said Mrs. Tillotson. "Hit's just what I been telling you, though nobody took the trouble to listen."

"I was listening real close," said Sam Tillotson from his corner.

No one paid attention. A babble of voices broke over the room. Everyone wanted to talk at once, everyone had an opinion about the letter. It was plain to all that Mr. Jason had sent it up the creek and that it had been delivered to Annie Lou. She had been sure that it was a Heaven-sent message from Mrs. Mather and had hidden the letter to keep it safe from harm.

The neighbors even spoke approvingly of Liza's part in finding the letter's long hiding place. Annie Lou was the only one who had nothing to say. She was too busy rearranging her treasures in the old rocker.

"Smart piece of thinking. Couldn't do better myself," said Mr. Bedford, nodding at Liza.

But Liza wasn't interested in praise. That could come later. Right now she wanted to know what the letter said. "Read it!" she shouted.

Dan Mather shook his head. He seemed almost stunned by the swift change and confusion about him. He turned his back on the crowded room. "You read it, Adam," he said hoarsely and held the letter toward Adam.

It was signed by Travis Barton. Liza saw his name at the bottom of the paper as she peered over Adam's elbow. The date was that of the month following her mother's death. It was not a long letter. It only said that Mr. Barton had received Mrs. Mather's letter and would look into the matter of a school for the Hundredfold at his earliest convenience.

That was all, but it was enough. It proved that Mrs. Mather had written to ask about the possibility of a school and that Mr. Barton thought her request worth his attention.

"I'm afraid it took me longer than I first hoped to come here and make the survey."

Mr. Barton was in the doorway. He came forward into the room and no one tried to stop him. Dan Mather did not appear to notice him. His back was still turned to the others.

"Survey?" Adam spoke huskily, but his eagerness was plain in his voice. "Do you think . . . will there be a school?"

"There will be one if your pa listens to reason," said Mrs. Tillotson, who had been left out of things long enough. "All the rest of us is agreed on the school and where it should stand. Its right and proper place is on that there bluff, smack in the middle of the area. Hit's the . . ."

"On the bluff!" cried Liza. The bluff was right at the edge of the Mather property. Everyone in the Hundredfold would come to the bluff to school and she would be in the midst of everything. "Father, do you hear? The school's going to be on the bluff!"

Dan Mather faced the room. He paid no attention to Liza or to any of the neighbors. He looked right at Mr. Barton.

"I have done you a wrong," he said slowly. "I ask your pardon." He jerked his head in a stiff nod.

"There's no need to apologize," said Mr. Barton. "I understand." He offered his hand to Dan Mather. "I'm glad to talk to you at last. I'd like to explain all this if I may." He looked once at Mrs. Tillotson, but she pretended to be fussing with one of the children who were clustered about her.

Someone pulled up a chair for Mr. Barton and seated him in the exact center of the room. Mrs. Tillotson stood by Sam's chair with her hand on his shoulder. He had been the only one who had listened to her and she was prepared to forgive him everything for that kindly act. The children sat on the floor as near their mother as they could get. Seth was with them. He was too fond of his playmates to want to leave them.

Emmy crept forward and sat on the hearth with Liza. Liza wanted to be close to Annie Lou in case she started her wild talk again. But Annie Lou showed no signs of interrupting. Now that she was no longer guardian of the message she seemed content to let it be in other hands. She sat among her treasures, rocking and humming to herself.

Even Mr. Bedford was quiet. He stood near the door with his thumbs over his belt, nodding agreement to all that Mr. Barton said. It was as though he had planned things to turn out as they had and took full credit for the listening attention of the room. Mr. Lasher stood beside him, nodding in time to the motions of Mr. Bedford's head.

Mr. Barton spoke slowly and carefully. He told how he had received Mrs. Mather's letter and how he had answered it. He explained that the State Department of Education, of which he was a member, wanted schools in all the remote areas of the state. First the Department had to be shown the need for such a school and Mrs. Mather had made that clear in her letter.

"Mrs. Mather must have been a remarkable woman," said Mr. Barton gently. "She told how she had taught her children to read but that she wanted them to have the advantage of a trained teacher."

Dan Mather sat with his head bowed. He did not look up.

Adam, who was standing close to Mr. Barton's chair, tightened his hands on the chair back. Liza stared at the floor. She thought of the hours her mother had spent teaching her to read and how she had neglected it in the past months. But Adam hadn't stopped his reading. She looked up and watched his face as Mr. Barton went on talking.

He explained his delay in coming to the Hundredfold. When he had at last found time from the press of other business he had arrived to find the area in a turmoil of unneighborliness. He had talked to the others, the Tillotsons, the Bedfords, and the Lashers. They all agreed that a school was needed and wanted. They had also decided that the bluff was the place for the school. It was in the center of the five-mile area that the school would serve. But until now it had been impossible to talk to Dan Mather about a school or anything else.

"Of course we shall need your permission to use the land on the bluff," said Mr. Barton. "It would be an ideal spot. It is high above flood level and . . ."

"Thanks be to the Devil's Seesaw," said Mr. Bedford loudly. "If that there stone wasn't laying where it is Dan Mather would be flooded out and likely the bluff too. Hit's nothing short of a miracle."

No one listened to Mr. Bedford. Everyone watched Dan Mather and waited for his word. Still he did not speak. His hand shaded his eyes and it was impossible to know what he was thinking.

"Will there be others outside our hollow coming to the school?" asked Liza when she could stay quiet no longer. She had to find out how many children might be coming to the bluff. Perhaps there would be strangers coming, girls she had never seen or known. They would be new people, different from Emmy. But even as she thought this Liza moved closer to Emmy. She would always be her first friend.

"About twenty in all, I figure," said Mr. Barton. "The bluff is the center of a five-mile radius, as I said, which makes a good school district. It must be within walking distance, of course. There are other things I must explain before Mr. Mather makes up his mind. The State undertakes to supply the teacher and the books. They . . ."

"Books!" Adam whispered the word.

"Oh yes. The textbooks and . . ."

"A dictionary book?" demanded Liza. She forgot it was rude to interrupt. The hope in Adam's eyes was almost too bright to bear.

Mr. Barton nodded.

"Then you won't have to save for it!" cried Liza. She beamed on Mr. Barton.

"There's only one difficulty," said Mr. Barton.

Everyone stiffened to attention. It was as though the room was holding its breath. Even Dan Mather watched Mr. Barton now.

"Provided Mr. Mather gives permission to use his land," said Mr. Barton, "there's the problem of building the school itself. This must be done by the people using the school. The lumber must be provided, the actual building erected, and money raised for desks, chairs, and such. Of course if Mr. Mather consents to provide the land he would not be asked to give money too. It would be more than his share to give the land."

Dan Mather cleared his throat. "There's no call for that," he said. "I can give my share of money. As for the bluff . . ." He stopped and looked out

202

through the open door toward the distant bluff. "It was a favorite place for my wife to walk," he said slowly. "I could wish she had a part in the school. It was her wish and desire."

"Schools has names," said Mrs. Tillotson briskly. "Name it for her. The Eliza Mather School, that's what, and a good name it is after a good woman."

Dan Mather looked at Mr. Barton. "Will it be so?" he asked.

Mr. Barton nodded. "The Eliza Mather School," he said.

Liza didn't pay much attention to the talk in the room after that. She saw Adam walk out to the porch and knew he wanted to be by himself so he could think of the school, the books, and the teacher. She hoped he was remembering that he wouldn't have to save for a dictionary book now.

She thought of the school too. She hoped the teacher would be nice. She even gave a quick thought to the books. But most of all she wondered about the new girls she would know, ones of her own age who liked to do what she did and were not afraid all the time. She patted Emmy's shoulder as this thought drifted into her mind.

The grown folk talked about lumber and building and money. There wasn't much cash money in the Hundredfold. It would have to be raised somehow and they talked about that. They spoke about the right way to cut trees for lumber, a few here and there on the mountain so as not to spoil the land.

Mr. Barton gave advice and listened. He was sure the money could be raised. All that was needed was the will and the effort. He was ready to help in any way he could.

"If the building can be finished this summer there is no reason why the school can't open this fall," said Mr. Barton. "The teacher and the books will be ready."

Adam had come back into the room to stand near his father. "This fall?" he asked. "You mean there will be books this fall?"

Mr. Bedford coughed to attract attention. "Takes a power of time to build," he said importantly. "Don't see as how we can get a school raised in that time. Got to get the lumber cut and sawed to start. Don't see as there'd be time afore fall."

"There's work in plenty for a man come summer," said Mr. Lasher. He looked startled when he finished speaking, as though surprised he had said anything at all.

"My leg being hurt bad won't hurry the work," said Sam Tillotson. He groaned and rubbed his injured leg. "I'm up to a power of work when I'm fitten, but . . ."

Liza wasn't listening any longer. She was watching Adam and the fading light in his eyes. She couldn't bear to see it. There must be some way to hurry the work. There had to be a school building ready in the fall for the teacher and the books.

"A working!" Liza leaped to her feet as the great idea came to her. It was like a flash of lightning in her brain from somewhere outside herself.

They all looked at her, but Liza didn't care. She was too full of her great idea. "Like the working on the Tillotsons' house," she said, her words falling over each other in her eagerness. "With everybody working together on the house it will be fixed right quick. There could be a working on the school, too, and it could be done in a day or a week or maybe a month." Her voice trailed off as her thought lengthened. "Anyway," she said, "there could be a working."

No one said anything for a long minute. Then her father touched her arm. "I'm agreeable," he said quietly. "For the Eliza Mather School there could be a working."

Liza let the others do the talking after that. There were plans and talk for an hour or more. The neighbors left at last and Mr. Barton with them. As he went out the door he looked back and smiled at Liza in a way that made her spirits leap. She knew he was telling her that it was her idea for the working that had made the building of the school a near reality.

The Tillotsons and the Mathers sat down to a

late dinner together. There was no room at the table for the young Tillotsons or Seth. They sat on the floor behind Mrs. Tillotson's chair and ate the best pieces of the fried pork and raised biscuits which she saved for them when she had served the grown folk.

Liza and Emmy were crowded together at one end of the table, but they didn't mind the lack of elbow room. They were sitting with the grown folk and eating from the china plates with the red roses and gold flecks. Annie Lou was at the table too. She had the place of honor beside Dan Mather, for she was old and it was her right to be shown respect.

Mrs. Tillotson did most of the talking. She made plans for the working on the school and she told everybody just how it should be done. If anyone else had ideas about the working they had no chance to mention them except during the short moments when Mrs. Tillotson had to stop and catch her breath.

". . . and once the lumber is cut and sawed to lengths, it can be stacked right on the bluff ready for the working. I reckon it will take . . ."

Liza stopped listening. She began thinking of the fun it would be to help with the sawing and the hammering as the school building was raised. She could hammer nails almost as well as Adam and she only hit her thumb once or twice when each nail was driven into place. She could help shingle the roof when the time came, for she was small and quick and could climb like a squirrel. There were a thousand things she could do for the working and Liza wanted to do them all.

". . . and us women folk, Emmy, Liza, and me, can set up a cooking fire right near the bluff and serve out the vittles. What with keeping the men folk fed and minding the young 'uns we'll have our work cut out for us. Hear, Emmy?"

"Yes'm," said Emmy.

"You hear, Liza?"

Liza heard but she couldn't answer. All her high hopes of helping at the working crashed into the dull duty of cooking and minding the children. She stared at the red roses on her plate.

"Well?" Mrs. Tillotson wanted an answer and now everyone at the table was looking at Liza and waiting too.

"I thought . . ." Liza stopped and began again. "There's things on the working I could do. I can hammer and . . ."

Dan Mather cleared his throat and Liza looked at him quickly. Both her father and Adam who sat near him were watching her. Adam lifted his eyebrows in a warning signal, but her father's face told her nothing of what he was thinking. Liza knew what he wanted. He wanted her to tell Mrs. Tillotson that she would help with the cooking and the children as a woman should. Liza took a long, unsteady breath. She remembered suddenly how it had been in the house the day she first brought out the china plates for her father and put the flowers on the table. Then she had acted as a woman should and the whole house and the people in it had been warmed and comforted by what she had done.

Slowly Liza nodded. "Yes'm," she said clearly.

Dan Mather cleared his throat again, this time with a sound that was almost a laugh. "Seems to me," he said, "there's work in plenty for some folks both with the cooking and with the building."

Liza almost jumped out of her chair. It didn't seem possible that her father could be saying the things she was hearing.

"I might be wrong," Dan Mather said, "but I hear it said that nowadays a girl can do 'most anything, some girls, that is."

"I can," said Liza breathlessly.

"Hammering and sawing and . . . and wearing a boy's pants."

Liza's face grew hot. She heard Mrs. Tillotson's scornful sniff and a faint sigh from Emmy. But she looked only at her father. He got up suddenly from the table and turned to Adam.

"So be it," said Dan Mather. "Adam, skirts has no place on a working. Next time you're at the

209

Crossings get pants for Liza. She's not to wear your old ones at the working."

"Father!" Liza's shriek of joy drowned out Mrs. Tillotson's disgusted snort and Annie Lou's disapproving murmurs. She threw herself at her father and hugged him hard.

"You mean I can wear 'em . . . the pants I mean . . . and help with the working?" Liza hugged him again.

"Hit'll be the ruination of her," said Mrs. Tillotson.

"Girls is girls and boys is boys," said Annie Lou warningly. She shook her head and mumbled to herself.

"That's what I mean," said Dan Mather, who wasn't listening to the woman-talk. "Adam, you hear me?"

"Yessir," said Adam and winked at Liza.

"You'll never be what your mother was," said Mrs. Tillotson, who had to say what she thought even when no one listened.

Dan Mather held Liza close to his side. "Maybe not," he said slowly, "but near enough to suit me."

"And that's enough for me," said Liza.